Voices of the Diaspora

VOICES OF THE
DIASPORA

*Jewish Women Writing
in Contemporary Europe*

EDITED BY THOMAS NOLDEN
AND FRANCES MALINO

NORTHWESTERN UNIVERSITY PRESS
Evanston, Illinois

Northwestern University Press
www.nupress.northwestern.edu

Printed in the United States of America

10 9 8 7 6 5 4 3 2 1

ISBN 0-8101-2221-9 (cloth)
ISBN 0-8101-2222-7 (paper)

Library of Congress Cataloging-in-Publication Data

Voices of the diaspora : Jewish women writing in contemporary Europe /
edited by Thomas Nolden and Frances Malino.
     p. cm. — (Jewish lives)
     Fiction and essays presented at two symposia held at Wellesley College,
Mass., in Apr. 1999 and in Stockholm in Feb. 2002.
     Includes bibliographical references.
     Text in English; translated from Dutch, French, German, Italian, Russian,
and Spanish.
     ISBN 0-8101-2221-9 (cloth : alk. paper) — ISBN 0-8101-2222-7 (pbk. :
alk. paper)
     1. Jewish fiction—20th century—Translations into English—Congresses.
2. Jewish fiction—Women authors—Translations into English—Congresses.
3. European fiction—Jewish authors—Translations into English—Congresses.
4. Jewish women—Europe—Social conditions—Fiction—Congresses.
5. Jewish women—Europe—Biography—Congresses. I. Nolden, Thomas.
II. Malino, Frances. III. Series.
PN6120.95.J6V65 2005
809.3'99287'089924—dc22

                                                                    2005001543

To the women whose voices were silenced

Contents

Reinvention

Introduction

Thomas Nolden

This anthology introduces the writing of contemporary Jewish women authors from Austria, France, Germany, Great Britain, Italy, the Netherlands, Russia, and Spain. Their works, written over the course of the last twenty-five years, represent an exciting facet of both contemporary culture in the new Europe and of Jewish life in the European Diaspora. The stories and essays compiled in this volume allow readers to appreciate the contribution of women writers to the reemergence of Jewish culture on the continent where the Jewish population was almost annihilated.

Half a decade after the Shoah, Jewish life in Europe, a continent which used to regard—and treat—the Jews as its Other, is astonishingly vivacious and diverse. It is the subject of heated debates about the relationship between Jewish identity and the spirit of the new Europe. Some observers, like the French philosopher Alexandre J.-L. Delamarre, are suggesting that Jews now serve as the "implicit model of European identity" (Delamarre, 96); others, like the British historian Bernard Wasserstein, proclaim the "vanishing" of the European Diaspora. What remains undisputable, however, is the fact that Europe has seen fundamental changes in the demography of its Jewish population. The former centers of Jewish life have shifted toward the West, and Eastern Europe is no longer home to the majority of Europe's Jews.

Before 1939, almost three and a half million Jews lived in the former USSR. After the war, the number had shrunk to fewer than two million, and following the end of the cold war, the Jewish population had dwindled in 1990 to just half of this figure. Approximately three and a quarter million Jews were living in Poland before the war; in 1990, there were merely some thirty-eight hundred Jews left.

At the beginning of the 1960s, decolonization in North Africa brought large numbers of Sephardic Jews to France, changing Europe's first emancipated Jewish community both in number and in nature. France now has Europe's largest Jewish community (with about 650,000 Jews), followed by Great Britain (approximately 315,000) and Germany (approximately 60,000). Hungary (approximately 55,000), Belgium (approximately 32,000), Italy (approximately 31,000), the Netherlands (approximately 26,000), Switzerland (approximately 19,000), Sweden (approximately 15,000), Spain (approximately 12,000), and Austria (approximately 7,000) follow in rank. There are almost two million Jews living in Europe, representing approximately 15 percent of the Jewish population of the entire world. Almost a fourth of all Jews living in the Diaspora reside in Europe.

To be sure, these figures pale in regard to the nine and a half million Jews who lived in Europe prior to the Shoah, and they point to the physical, emotional, and cultural devastation Europe's Jews had to endure. But to infer from the statistics simply that European Jewry is a phenomenon of the past would be to ignore the presence of its culture, which continues to prosper and flourish.

The end of the cold war and the demise of grand ideological master narratives, the effects of global migration, and the emerging self-assertion of ethnic and religious minorities have altered formerly monocultural and monoreligious European societies. Such changes have energized a trend toward disassimilation, which can be witnessed in virtually all of Europe's Jewish communities. This anthology would like to serve as a vade mecum to understand, from the specific point of view of women writers, where these communities have come from, how they have dealt with the ruptures of near annihilation and displacement, and how they envision their futures in a Europe whose many transformations have not rooted out anti-Semitism altogether.

In focusing our collection on the works of women writers, we present a segment of contemporary Jewish European culture usually overshadowed by the "grand old men" of Jewish letters. The books of Primo Levi (Italy), Imre Kertész (Hungary), André Schwarz-Bart and Marek Halter (France), Jurek Becker (Germany [East Berlin]), and Henryk Grynberg (Poland) can be found easily in bookstores, and their immense accomplishments have been appreciated and studied all over the world. The works of their female colleagues, however, are hardly known beyond the borders of the countries in which these women writers reside, and most of them did not even know about each other until a symposium on Jewish women writers in the new Europe brought some of them together, first in New England and later in Stockholm, Sweden.[1] This volume seeks to offer a forum for their stories so that they can share them with an audience already familiar with Jewish women writers of an older generation and of different national backgrounds. This forum will allow us to grasp the contours of a literature that shares, beyond the gender of its authors, several points of departure and important stylistic and thematic features, despite the differences of the vernaculars in which individual works have been conceived and the national and historical contexts in which they have emerged.

Jewish women's writing from Europe is not entirely unknown to American audiences. Anne Frank's *Diary of a Young Girl* has been enormously popular since its first publication in 1947. Not surprisingly, the diary has been read not merely as a historical document but also—even primarily—as a piece of literature that offers a "great source of comfort and support" (as Frank writes in her opening entry) the way powerful literary texts do. Another author whose name still resonates with contemporary readers is the German-language writer Nelly Sachs (1891–1970). Together with the Israeli author Shmuel Yosef Agnon,

Sachs in 1966 received the Nobel Prize for literature in recognition of the powerful poetic language she crafted to commemorate the suffering of her people during her exile in Sweden.

The memoirs of women who have survived the Shoah continue to capture our attention. Ruth Klüger articulates in her prizewinning autobiography, *Still Alive: A Holocaust Girlhood Remembered* (2001), one of the objectives that lies at the core of Jewish women's writing:

> Yet I am often told that I underestimate the role of woman in Judaism. She may light the Sabbath candles after having set the table, an important function. I don't want to set the Sabbath table or light candles; I don't live with tablecloths and silverware. And why do you want to say kaddish? the same people, who know me, ask in astonishment. We haven't seen you pray a lot, nor do you wear sackcloth and ashes in public. True, true, but the dead set us certain tasks, don't they? They want to be remembered and revered, they want to be resurrected and buried at the same time. I want to say kaddish because I live with the dead. If I can't do that, forget about religion. Poetry is more helpful. (Klüger, 30–31)

The passage expresses the desire of the woman writer to share positions of articulation and forms of participation that Judaism traditionally has reserved for men. Klüger claims poetry—and writing in general—as a medium of articulation of women's voices. As Klüger's reference to the kaddish suggests, they do not necessarily want to express dissent. They sometimes simply want to join in the textual rituals that tradition has reserved for men, especially when following the biblical imperative *Zakhor!* The command to remember has been a powerful vector directing Jewish writers of both genders to the past of the Jewish people, to the commemoration of the dead.

Our anthology shifts the center of attention to writers in the generations after those of Nelly Sachs, Anne Frank, and Ruth Klüger. In doing so, this collection introduces forms of Jewish women's writing that not only complement certain traditions of Judaism but also engage in critical commentary and reflection on the past and the present of the Jewish experience from the perspective of women. Even the publication history of Anne Frank's famous diary indicates that such a perspective tends to be neglected or even consciously omitted. For decades, Frank's diary was subjected to editors erasing the passages that spoke specifically to the writer's experience as a woman—her relationship to her mother, her sexuality, her "observations of the misogyny of her society" (Bernard, 216)—because they favored a text that suggested the self-portrayal of a childlike, or genderless, victim.

The majority of authors assembled in this volume were born after the Shoah. Michelene Wandor was born during the war, and Ludmila Ulitskaya and Myriam Anissimov toward its end. Such an accentuation allows us to discern the concerns of literature written by Jewish women belonging to the second and third generations after the Shoah. This anthology thus addresses not only and not primarily the experience of surviving the Shoah. It accentuates a literature that speaks to the experience of women growing up on a continent whose Jewish communities had nearly been destroyed and which have had to undergo difficult processes of reconstruction, integration, and displacement, including the uprooting of thousands of Sephardic Jews following the independence movements of Tunisia and Morocco in 1956 and of Algeria in 1962.

These women write as daughters of parents who were murdered or who found ways of surviving or resisting; as women who could make choices that history and tradition had not afforded their predecessors; as citizens of countries that only slowly have come to acknowledge their guilt for the crimes against their Jewish compatriots; or as citizens of countries that tried to fight the deportation of their Jewish population. They write as former students of Karl Marx and, at times, of the Talmud and, in almost all cases, of Simone de Beauvoir's feminist study *The Second Sex.*

Writing from the Margins

> There feels at the moment to be a way in which three marginalized
> voices, voices from exile, Jewish, woman and feminist, can make
> sense in relation to a dominant voice. (Wandor 1986, 85)

The British Jewish writer Michelene Wandor here alludes to a
unique constellation that at the end of the 1970s and the beginning of the 1980s led to the emergence of contemporary Jewish
women's writing. Certainly, there had been—as modern theory
would call it—"extraterritorial" writing before that point in
time: one only has to think of the many émigré writers desper-
ately looking for refuge from the Nazis. Many of them were of
Jewish descent, and many of them were women. And yet the peculiar confluence of factors to which Wandor alludes differs dra-
matically from earlier constellations: only during the latter half
of the twentieth century did a critical number of women authors
consciously embrace all three of these accidental features of their
existence as substantive, constitutive elements of their artistic
identity. In their writing they want to explore fully the attri-
butes of Judaism, woman, and exile/Diaspora and to examine
how these conditions relate to each other as well as to a culture
dominated by non-Jewish males.

These women writers concerned themselves explicitly with
Jewish matters and with the experience of the Jewish people,
thus setting themselves apart from those of their colleagues who
had tended to refrain in their works from referring to their ethnic heritage. This discreetness about Jewish roots pertains to such
internationally renowned writers as Nathalie Sarraute (1900–
99), who headed the French school of the New Novelist, and
Anita Brookner (born 1928), the prolific British novelist, to
name but two of the most famous cases. A long list of male coun-
terparts might also be added.

There are manifold reasons why many of the older writers of
Jewish background—and also some of the younger contemporary ones—do not want to be perceived as Jewish writers despite

their Jewish background. A long history of acculturation may have separated them from their ethnic background; the power of secularization may have estranged them from the religious beliefs of their ancestors. Leftist doctrines, often following the traditions of humanist optimism, challenged many of them to, in Natalia Ginzburg's words, "transcend the limitations of one's heritage" and to speak from a position beyond nationality, religion, and ethnicity. Aesthetic programs, often following the traditions of Enlightenment cosmopolitanism, charged some of them to create a voice that transcended the particular and strove for the universal. But there also has been the fear of repercussions from audiences who did not want to be reminded of their complicity in discriminating against or persecuting Jewish compatriots and the fear of sanctions by publishing houses not interested in Jewish literature. And, last but not least, there has been the fear of being harassed and persecuted by governments that, as in the case of the Soviet Union, engaged in anti-Semitic purges through the early 1950s or by Islamic independence movements, as in the case of some of the French colonies and territories in North Africa during decolonization.

In spite of vastly different national, cultural, and historical backgrounds, these writers nonetheless all took advantage of a movement beginning in the late 1970s and early 1980s that allowed European Jews to gain a new appreciation of their Jewish heritage. No longer preoccupied with the ideological battles that had been fought in the previous decades, they now could express and explore this renewed appreciation in a manner unheard of in earlier times. These authors are our contemporaries. Their experience includes the loss of family members and of places their parents called home but also the establishment of a Jewish state (the politics of which they may at times oppose) and an awareness of the persecution of peoples belonging to other religious and ethnic groups or to dissenting political parties. These authors did not settle in Israel but instead have stayed in Gentile countries in which they or their ancestors had settled. They have spent their formative years in an era that brought about po-

liticalization and ideological polarization and that has created a
new consciousness of the rights and roles of women.

Points of Departures

Growing up in societies that only very reluctantly began to acknowledge the fate of their Jewish populations during World
War II, the children of survivors rarely experienced a vibrant Jewish culture or religious devotion; most instead faced a twofold
silence. In both Germanies, and initially also in Italy, France,
Hungary, Poland, and the Soviet Union, anti-Semitic perpetra-
tors deliberately obscured their crimes by enforcing silence. Survivors themselves often felt voiceless: the paralyzing effects of
their own trauma and their guilt at surviving while so many others had died left them unable to break the silence imposed upon
them. Born during or after the war, most Jews grew up in what
David Rousset called in 1945 *l'univers concentrationaire*—in families that had been truncated and shaken by the genocide, in
which the Shoah was not just a singular event but an ongoing
force of emotional destruction that often was too difficult for the
survivors, the parents, to articulate. To be sure, however, this did
not mean that it was not communicated without words or that
it did not have a major impact on the following generations.

   To rediscover their ties to the Jewish past and tradition, the
young Jews in West Germany, France, and Italy have had to
overcome barriers set up by their societies' reluctance to address
the fate of the Jews during National Socialism, Vichy collabora-
tion, and Fascism. They also have had to overcome the barriers
set up by their own politics. The political imperative of the re-
bellious era of the student revolution was to put the cause of in-
ternationalism above ethnic (not to mention Zionist) concerns,
leading many young Jews in Europe to ignore the little they
knew about their roots. The initial wave of politicization in the
late 1960s and the 1970s left little space for the exploration of
ethnic, religious, regional, and cultural differences. After all,

Marxism insisted that any affiliation other than solidarity with the working class was tantamount to false consciousness, a remnant of bourgeois ideology.

Thus, many young Jews could reconnect to their ethnic and cultural heritage once the student rebellion had reached its ideological climax and opened up space for discussions in which the notion of identity was no longer defined solely by class. At that juncture younger Jews no longer concealed their curiosity about the path Jewish culture and Judaism had taken in the United States, where a multitude of voices had created different strands of Jewish identities and communities and had started to become an important feature of contemporary culture. What earlier had been denounced as a category of the accidental and subjective now was embraced as a particularity worth exploring.

In Eastern Europe, the dynamics of societal discourse and identity politics undoubtedly took a different path after the end of the war, and yet the stories we learn from Jews growing up in this part of the Diaspora are not entirely dissimilar to the experiences of their Western peers. Communist governments were interested in portraying Communists as the real victims of Fascism. They downplayed the persecution of the Jews, who would often continue to find themselves on the list of unwanted citizens. Many Jews had envisioned these Communist countries to be safe havens in which ethnic and religious differences among the citizens would be of no importance whatsoever—an illusion that often ran into the dead end of anti-Semitic campaigns.

The Hungarian-born economist Eva Szita-Morris wrote in 1998 about the rejuvenation of Judaism in Hungary following the end of the cold war:

> The Holocaust has had its delayed effects: it caused, and is causing, irreparable damage to those people and their children who decided to try silent coexistence in a society which had previously betrayed and rejected them and later sentenced them to death. Its inherent anti-Semitism coupled with the socialist system merely added to this burden.

The war and postwar history of Hungarian Jews is, par excellence, that of the outsider: the exiled, the left out, and of those who had internalized this alienation. Assimilation, because it deprived us of memory and self-understanding, made us outsiders to ourselves. Our parents and, until now, we ourselves excluded ourselves or were excluded from our real selves, from a possible social, cultural, historical experience.

We are now gaining back our parents. They are at last speaking with us. The internalized denial of their Jewish identity, the burden which they took on their shoulders after the war, that is, the decision to pursue the path of assimilation as though nothing had happened, is slowly being lightened. (Szita-Morris, 56)

In her book *Eine Liebe aus Nichts* (*A Love out of Nothing*, 1991), Barbara Honigmann addresses the same phenomenon and seeks to understand why her parents and those of her peers had remained so silent about their past. Honigmann was born in 1949 in East Berlin to parents who, having left Nazi Germany for England, returned after the war to help build what was supposed to become a Communist society free of prejudice and racism:

My parents even could say that they had been lucky, but for the rest of this life they had to live with the images and accounts of those who had no luck at all, and that must have been a big burden, so big that they always pretended that they had nothing to do with it and that nobody ever had belonged to them who had died a wretched death in a ghetto or who had been gassed in Auschwitz. . . . And finally, they had come to Berlin to build a new Germany, which was supposed to be completely different from the old one; therefore they preferred not to talk about the Jews at all. (Honigmann, 34)

Learning from the disillusionment of their parents, whose ideals eventually would collapse with the fall of the Berlin wall, the younger generation of Jews shed obsolete and stifling templates of identity. Jean-Paul Sartre's influential idea that Jewish identity consists solely of a projection of the anti-Semite was dismissed and with it the persona of the invisible Jew who had managed to hold on to the ideal of acculturation despite Europe's betrayal of its Jewish citizens.

Opening Lines

It is not uncommon to find among Europe's Jewish writers a biographical pattern that shows a deep split in their careers, separating their works into an early phase, in which references to Jewish matters are entirely absent, and a "second act," in which a strong concern for the past and present of the Jewish experience suddenly features strongly. This pattern documents the fault line that ran through the late 1970s and the early 1980s, effecting a fundamental break in the biographies of so many second-generation Jews in Europe. For example, at the beginning of Warsaw-born writer Hanna Krall's publishing career are books that do not at all relate to her experience of surviving the war in hiding while her entire family was murdered in the Majdanek death camp. In 1977, however, she published her famous portrait of the last survivor of the Jewish Fighting Organization in the Warsaw ghetto, Marek Edelman. In 1985, having achieved enough distance from the traumatic events that had shaped her own life, Krall published her first novel, *The Subtenant*. The autobiographically informed account leads from years of hiding to the eventual creation of the antigovernment Solidarnosc movement. First published in France, the novel was for many years itself something of a clandestine "subtenant" of Polish letters.

Compared to Hanna Krall, born in 1937, the writers featured in our anthology are more removed from the trauma of persecution and faced aesthetic challenges different from those of the survivors. Their relative distance from the events that had shattered the lives of the older Jews allowed them to approach the Jewish experience of the twentieth century much more directly. The two youngest authors introduced in our anthology, Ruth Beckermann from Austria and Carl Friedman from the Netherlands, both set out in their careers as writers (or, in Beckermann's case, as a documentary filmmaker) to speak directly to the past and present of Jewish life. Beckermann researched the lost legacy of Jewish culture in her native Austria, and Carl Friedman's first novel, *Nightfather* (1991), sketches a moving portrait of a father returning to the Netherlands from the concentration camps. These younger authors started writing in societal contexts that, due in part to the efforts of their older colleagues, had become more open to minority voices. They often grew up in Jewish contexts characterized by a self-assertiveness only rarely found in the immediate postwar years: Friedman's portrayal of the surviving father who is constantly alluding to his suffering in the concentration camps is rendered with a great deal of sympathy—and with a humor almost unfathomable in a narrative on survivors a decade earlier. Her story "Holy Fire," featured in our anthology, will give the readers a taste of Friedman's penchant for tragicomedy.

Regardless of whether these writers started out addressing Jewish matters or not, they have all been influenced by the aesthetic idioms and literary styles prevalent in the national literatures of the countries in which they reside. It would make little sense to assume that a Jewish writer would subscribe solely to the tradition of Jewish literature rather than exposing herself to the confluence of literary styles and idioms that make up cultural life in the Diaspora. Just as women authors in general are, according to the feminist literary critic Elaine Showalter, not both "*inside* and *outside* of the male tradition but inside two traditions simultaneously" (Showalter, 264), Jewish writers partake of literary movements and find themselves in literary traditions whose histories sometimes are difficult to reconcile with the past of the Jewish people. Thus, it is a double "doubleness" that characterizes the position of these writers. The Spanish-language writer Reina Roffé cannot but be aware of the powerful impact exerted by the stylistics of magical realism, the prominence of which is strongly tied to Catholic culture. Barbara Honigmann, to name another example, acknowledges that her oeuvre resonates with the prose of German classicism and romanticism, and the Algerian-born writer Marlène Amar insists that "my culture is first and foremost French."[2] Eva Kuryluk (born in Krakow in 1946), to give yet another example, turns this multiple allegiance to various cultural traditions into a postmodern cultural cosmopolitanism: the protagonist of her novel *Century 21* encounters Anna Karenina and Simone Weil, Joseph Conrad and Malcolm Lowry, Djuna Barnes and Moses Maimonides.

And yet while actively and successfully partaking in cultural contexts at large, these writers relate consciously to the Jewish experience as a core feature of their literary imagination. These references can take on all sorts of different forms. They can consist, for example, of allusions to the literary canon of Jewish writing of the past, to figures from the Hebrew Bible, or to events in the history of Jewish people. When the French Jewish writer Myriam Anissimov, the daughter of a Yiddish-language poet, declares herself a "Yiddish writer who writes in French," she situates herself in a linguistic and literary tradition whose disappearance continues to pain her. Hanna Krall alludes in her works to biblical figures and constellations in her documentary pieces on the relationship of Jews, Poles, and Germans, Carl Friedman intersperses her stories and novels with references to medieval Jewish poetry, and Sylvie Weil devotes an entire novel to the life of Rashi. Her colleague Anne Rabinovitch revisits in her novels the sites of the concentration camps, Eliette Abécassis depicts the Orthodox quarters of Jerusalem, while the British Jewish author Linda Grant has the protagonist of one of her novels bid farewell to her native England to set out for Palestine in pursuit of her desire to live in "modern times."

Writing in the Diaspora

How can we sing our songs in a foreign land? This question has been posed, as the literary critic Geoffrey Hartman reminds us, "since the Babylonian exile" (Hartman, 205). While each writer's work represents a more or less direct response to this core question, these responses are usually difficult to translate into conceptual language. Rejecting the centrality of a Jewish homeland or questioning the importance of a Jewish language for Jewish writing, some authors even reject the notion of Diaspora altogether. Others find themselves in multiple diasporas, relating their identity not only (or not primarily) to Israel but to homelands they or their parents had to give up: to the *mellahs* or the *haras,* the Jewish ghettos in the Maghreb, which the writer Marlène Amar had to leave for Paris, or to the dictatorship-ridden countries in Latin America like Argentina, from which Reina Roffé immigrated to Spain. Jewish writing in the Diaspora, then, is a complex endeavor that often is born out of difficult choices and multiple cultural allegiances and that has to deal with different sets of cultural contradictions and historical dilemmas.

The emergence of Jewish writing in the Diaspora has been accompanied by debates that articulated both the reservations this literature had to surmount as well as the hopes and expectations invested in it. At one extreme we find a school of thought that doubts the legitimacy, if not the possibility, of a genuine form of Jewish writing outside Israel and in a non-Jewish language. Those at the other end of the spectrum insist that the Diaspora is one of the most productive—and most common—modes of Jewish existence and therefore a fertile ground for artistic expression.

In her famous speech titled "Toward a New Yiddish," the American Jewish writer and critic Cynthia Ozick suggested in 1970 that

> nothing thought or written in Diaspora has ever been able to last unless it has been centrally Jewish. If it is centrally Jewish, it will last for Jews. If it is not centrally Jewish, it will last neither for the Jews nor for the host nations. Rashi lasts and Yehuda Halevi lasts. . . .
>
> By "centrally Jewish" I mean, for literature, whatever touches upon the liturgical. Obviously it does not refer only to prayer. It refers to a type of literature and to a type of perception. There is a critical difference between liturgy and a poem. Liturgy is in command of the reciprocal imagination rather than of the isolated lyri-

cal imagination. A poem is private flattery: it moves the private
heart, but to no end other than being moved. . . . Liturgy is also a
poem, but it is meant not to have only a private voice. Liturgy has
a choral voice, a communal voice: the echo of the voice of the Lord
of History. In all of history the literature that has lasted for Jews has
been liturgical. The secular Jew is a figment: when a Jew becomes
a secular person he is no longer a Jew. This is especially true for
makers of literature. (Ozick, 168–69)

Ozick introduced the notion of a "New Yiddish," which—as a
successor to Yiddish and Ladino as the great languages of the Diaspora—was supposed to develop especially in the United States
as a literary vessel for a new liturgical culture that among American Jews was rapidly burgeoning as the result of the Holocaust
and "of the restoration of Israel" (173). Taking advantage of her
right as a poet, Ozick offered the following comparison:

> A liturgical literature has the configuration of the ram's horn: you
> give strength to the inch-hole and the splendor spreads wide. A
> Jewish liturgical literature gives its strength to its peoplehood and
> the whole human note is heard everywhere, enlarged. The liturgi-
> cal literature produced by New Yiddish may include a religious
> consciousness, but it will not generally be religious in any explicit
> sense. . . . It will be touched by the Covenant. (Ozick, 174–75)

Using religious language and concepts derived from Jewish ritual, Ozick intriguingly moved the concept of the liturgical into
the very realm of the secular that she earlier had questioned as
legitimate grounds for the Jewish imagination. Whether one
agrees with her thinking or not—Ozick herself has since changed
her position vis-à-vis writing in the Diaspora—she was right in
drawing attention to a cultural phenomenon that indeed heralded the rejuvenation of a new Jewish literature. Writers like
Saul Bellow, Philip Roth, Joseph Heller, and herself had produced literary idioms that set their works strikingly apart from
the novels produced by their non-Jewish peers.

In Europe, however, the development of a new wave of Jewish writing would not occur until much later. Here, the debates predating the creation of young Jewish literature (*junge jüdische Literatur*) in Germany and Austria or new Jewish literature (*nouvelle littérature juive*) in France had articulated different positions. The famous dictum by the German Jewish philosopher Theodor W. Adorno according to which writing poetry after Auschwitz is an act of barbarism threatened in the early 1950s to silence the voices of the few survivors (reading the sparse poetry of Paul Celan, another German-language émigré, Adorno would soon change his position). Just a few years later, the Tunisian-born French writer Albert Memmi argued that a literary work can be called a piece of Jewish literature only if it takes into account the author's *condition juive*. Since the Jewish condition, in Memmi's view, is marked primarily by oppression and since Gentile readers are not at all interested in learning about this experience, Jewish writers find themselves stripped of a real foundation for their work. Thus, Memmi set his hopes for the development of a national Jewish literature: only Israel provides a language common to the authors and their Jewish readers, and only Israel allows for a Jewish identity that is not based in persecution and marginalization.

Contradicting the idea that Jewish writing could prosper only in Israel, the British critic, novelist, and essayist George Steiner promoted in 1985 in his seminal essay "Our Homeland, the Text" the notion that the text is the true Jewish homeland. The "locus of truth," Steiner postulates, "is always extraterritorial" (Steiner, 21). Following the notion prepared by the German Jewish Romantic Heinrich Heine, who in French exile had pronounced that for him Judaism was *das aufgeschriebene Vaterland* (the written homeland), Steiner elaborates:

> But when the text *is* the homeland, even when it is rooted only in the exact remembrance and seeking of a handful of wanderers, nomads of the word, it cannot be extinguished. Time is truth's passport and its native ground. What better lodging for the Jew? (Steiner, 24–25)

A Sephardic voice joined Steiner's emphatic endorsement of Diasporic culture: reflecting on his own nomadic experience, the Cairo-born Jewish philosopher Edmond Jabès (who died in 1991 in France) proposed that the only place inhabited by the Jew is the book, where the Jew "finds himself, in the book he questions himself, in the book he has his freedom, which has been forbidden him everywhere" (Jabès, 254).

Needless to say, the authors represented in our anthology—many of whom have been translated into Hebrew—all subscribe to the possibility of participating in the long history of Jewish writing from a Diasporic position. This position appears to be not only a motif of Jewish writing but perhaps one of its constitutive conditions.

Women Writing in the Diaspora

The anthropologist James Clifford summed up his groundbreaking research on Diasporic communities by stating, "Diasporic experiences are always gendered" (Clifford, 313). This observation opens up important avenues toward the literature presented in this volume. The Sephardic women writers who had left the Jewish ghettos of the Maghreb to settle in the Western metropolises document the many transformations this form of displacement has brought about for women in particular. Marlène Amar's novel *La femme sans tête* (*The Woman without a Head,* 1993) records the dissolution of the emotional and physical identity of a Sephardic immigrant from Algeria, who with the aid of cosmetic surgery alters her appearance to efface all traces of her North African origin:

> My sister, in transforming herself, ended up being the real thing. More French than nature itself. Today, she reads the New Testament and says "*Israélite*" when speaking of a Jew. (Amar, 96)

The effacement of the Sephardic self in the French Diaspora invites the comparison to the metamorphosis that leads to the loss of Gregor Samsa's identity in Franz Kafka's famous story. Amar reappropriates Kafka's parable of a young man's transformation by tracing the process by which the face, faith, and personality of a North African woman are irrevocably altered.

But Amar and many of her peers also chronicle the liberation experienced by many immigrant women when leaving behind the patriarchal structures of North African societies at large and their Jewish communities in particular. In her autobiographical essay "My Algeriance: In Other Words, to Depart Not to Arrive from Algeria," the writer and philosopher Hélène Cixous (born 1937) calls the Algeria of her childhood firmly "enemy of women" (Cixous, 272). Her francophone compatriots Annie Goldmann, Katia Rubinstein, Paule Darmon, Annie Fitoussi, and Chochana Boukhobza all describe in their fiction how immigration to Europe allowed them to exchange stifling codes of female behavior for a freedom of expression rather foreign to their native surroundings. They subtly negotiate the ambiguities inherent in their experiences of displacement and emancipation as Sephardic women in postcolonial France without succumbing to the temptations of acculturation or of nostalgia for the lost world of Maghrebi Judaism.

The liberating effect of displacement, however, is not unique to migration from North Africa to Europe's capitals. Barbara Honigmann's departure from East Berlin to Strasbourg, France, too, was a move that freed her from legacies that tended to silence women's voices. The self-imposed exile also enabled her to shed her role of muse for male peers back in Berlin's theaters and to become a writer on her own. At the same time, it led her out of a family history of acculturation and out of the "negative symbiosis" in which Germans and Jews had found themselves since the end of the war. And it afforded her access to a vital community of Orthodox Jewish learning that at the time of her departure could not be found in Germany.

Reina Roffé's story "Exotic Birds" (included in this anthology) presents yet another attitude toward a former center of Jewish life. While the main character seems "interested only in the port where the Sephardic Jews from Morocco used to disembark, among them her own young parents, who arrived at the beginning of the century," the narrator (the main character's niece) is rather uneasy about her aunt's "withdrawal into herself that made her invisible to everyone else." Sympathy draws the younger narrator to the peculiarly passive life of her relative, and she tries to understand the growing compliancy of the older woman kept in place by the "domineering men of the house." The narrator uses her words while her aunt hides herself in silence. She utters her words in exile, far away from the house that had no salvation to offer and that the older one did not ever manage to leave. Only the distance from home, the story seems to suggest, allows the woman to speak.

"Beyond the Bridges," the essay by the Austrian writer and filmmaker Ruth Beckermann reprinted in this anthology, illustrates that Diasporic experience can sometimes even be measured in yards and does not have to entail the crossing of national borders or continents. To tell the story of the old Jewish district of her native Vienna, she has to set out like a historian or a researcher, because she—like most of her peers—is not at all familiar with this aspect of her people's and her city's past: "We, the children of survivors, knew nothing at all. In conversations with Jews born after World War II in Vienna, you can frequently hear statements like 'My childhood was spent in a no-man's-land' or 'We did and did not live here.'" Beckermann's essay does not foreground the vicissitudes in the lives of the female inhabitants of the so-called Matzoh Island in the middle of the Danube River. In this respect, her piece differs from most of the other texts included in our anthology, which revisit the legacies of the experience of Jewish women in the European Diaspora.

Jewish Women Writing

Coining the term *Juifemme,* Hélène Cixous condensed into one word the spheres of personal (I; in French *je*), ethnic (Jewish; in

French *Juif*), and gender experience (woman; in French *femme*). None of these, the neologism suggests, can be separated from each other; intricately woven together, they inform the way Jewish women writers look at events in history and experience the present. Accordingly, most authors represented in our anthology have from the beginning of their careers concerned themselves with the experience of Jewish women.

In her first novel, *Comment va Rachel?* (*How Is Rachel?* 1973), Myriam Anissimov diagnoses the severe emotional disorder and utter despair brought upon a young Jewish woman by a feeling of profound humiliation. A photograph of a group of women smiling sadly in the Warsaw ghetto gains considerable importance for the protagonist—the daughter of a tailor who escaped persecution—who considers committing suicide by turning on the gas. Anissimov's book heralded Jewish women's writing by second-generation authors in France and is a remarkable document of the emotional syndrome that affected the life of many second-generation Jews. The book also made its mark as a counterpart to the American Jewish novel of the 1960s and 1970s, as it put on a map crowded with sexually obsessive middle-aged men the subtle portrayal of a mistreated young woman. In her very outspoken presentation of the sexual and emotional relationships between men and women, Anissimov stripped from this favorite theme of French literature the illusion of an equal distribution of roles and power between the sexes.

Her most recent novel, *Sa Majesté la mort* (*His Majesty, Death,* 1999), may be seen as a commissioned piece, apparently instigated by the author's mother: "She decided that I would be the guardian of her memory, of the memory of all of her people; the living and the dead" (Anissimov, 15). And yet the daughter does not simply reduce her own role to that of an archivist preserving a past that otherwise would fall prey to oblivion. The daughter-narrator instead establishes from the beginning her own place in her family's history. Remembering, then, is only one objective. The writer looks back also "in order not to feel a dreadful solitude" (30).

Coming from a very different angle and using a very different stylistic vocabulary, the British Jewish author Michelene Wandor returns to the biblical figure of Lilith, rescuing her not so much from historical oblivion as from misogynist misreadings. In her cycle of Lilith and Eve poems, Wandor introduces Adam's wife as a femme fatale powering the British women's liberation movement, for which Wandor in 1972 had prepared one of the founding documents (an essay collection titled *The Body Politic*). Wandor's Lilith insists "women fight, women prophesy, women lead, women judge" (Wandor 1999, 12) and accordingly engages in dialogue with Eve, the Lord, Job, and a female pope, or Persephone; she also comments on Jewish law. The poem "Lilith Re-tells Esther's Story" ends with a stanza that shows that Wandor's feminist reading of the scriptures goes beyond the interest of simply rediscovering strong Jewish women:

> there is something missing
> from this story:
> someone
> somewhere
> doesn't bother to say
> whether Esther
> actually liked
> King A (25)

Pointing out how textual traditions have tried to tame women by stripping them of their desires and holding up icons of exemplary Jewish womanhood, Wandor insists in her portraits of Jewish women that sexual desires indeed heed no boundaries, neither ethnic nor national ones. In her story "Song of the Jewish Princess," included in our volume, a Jewish woman troubadour fleeing the Spanish Inquisition resolutely succeeds Lilith in her pursuit of a life free from the conventions erected by men to rule women.

No such programmatic feminist overtones can be heard in the story "Jews" (translated for our anthology) by the Italian Jewish

writer Clara Sereni. The story, set in Fascist Italy, traces the bud-
ding friendship with a Jewish adolescent girl who brightens the
everyday life of a non-Jewish girl who leads a highly sheltered
middle-class life and who remains unnamed throughout the
entire story. When the Jewish classmate suddenly disappears
because she is no longer permitted to attend public school, her
friend withdraws disappointedly into herself. There are only faint
references to the persecution of Italian Jews under Mussolini.
Sereni has switched the narrative perspective prevalent in so
many texts by Jewish writers to tell the story from the angle of
the non-Jewish girl. With the allusions to the girl's difficulty in
creating intimate bonds, her admiration for the self-confidence
of the Jewish girlfriend, and with the authorial decision to model
the two girls as "twins," Sereni offers an intriguing picture of the
narcissistic psyche of Italy's Gentile middle class. Too preoccupied with themselves to save their Jewish compatriots, this
group ultimately experiences the suffering of the Jews as a personal crisis in which the Jews are blamed for upsetting a fragile
emotional balance. Two generations later, Jews reemerge in Italy
with a self-assertiveness that troubles a society that has found
comfort in amnesia.

Female Resistance

Many of the stories told by contemporary Jewish women writers
are narratives of female defiance and resistance. This is not to say
that there is a tendency toward hagiography in this literature or
that it focuses on the courageous deeds of women fighting their
persecutors in the ghettos or the concentration camps. The acts of
defiance chronicled by these women writers take different forms.

The Russian Jewish writer Ludmila Ulitskaya, in "March
1953," tells the story of a young Jewish girl growing up in the
house of her grandparents and her great-grandfather. The great-
grandfather early on initiates the child into the legacy of Jewish
resistance by sharing with her the stories of the biblical heroes

Daniel and Gideon. This generational setup is not accidental. Adhering to the religious tradition, the oldest living member of Lily's family can instill in the offspring the spirit to act that her grandparents—secular Jews with scientific training—cannot because they have lost faith and memory. Ulitskaya's story is a modern Purim story set on the eve of Stalin's death in March 1953; her unlikely heroine is a pubescent girl hardly aware of her people's fear of anti-Semitic purges by the government. Lily has to fight another enemy, a boy her own age who harasses her, casting himself grandiosely in the pose of Christ.

The symmetry of the narrative—Ulitskaya herself is, like Lily's grandparents, a trained scientist who believes in structure—has the anti-Semitic dictator (Stalin) and his Jewish opponent (the great-grandfather) take leave of their lives almost simultaneously, coinciding with Lily's confrontation with her offender.

Both Sereni and Ulitskaya allude in their stories to the awakening sexuality of their protagonists: it is the drama of physical attraction in which they find themselves entangled with their peers and antagonists. Ulitskaya's heroine is "on the threshold of puberty" when she fights her assailant: female autonomy and Jewish resistance here become almost identified with each other—and so is male violence and anti-Semitism.

The heroine of Michelene Wandor's "Song of the Jewish Princess" is a minstrel who tries to remain true to herself in a world hostile to Jews and women. Expelled from Spain in 1492, she finds refuge in the court of a northern Italian nobleman. Fully aware of the lethal consequences of her actions, Isabella betrays her husband with the man she really loves. Her confession "My text comes from the heart. Nothing can be more authentic" suggests that Wandor portrays, aside from the vicissitudes in the life of an uncompromising woman, the story of an artist who knows that her work rings true only when speaking from the heart, free of any constraints imposed on her. It is intriguing to see how Wandor's wandering artist's words correspond to George Steiner's caution that Jewish writing in the Diaspora must not submit to any territorial authority, including the one of the Promised Land: "Locked materially in a material homeland, the text may, in fact, lose its life-force, and its truth values may be betrayed" (Steiner, 24).

Reinventing Traditions

Despite its very richness and long-standing tradition, the history of Jewish women's writing has yet to be recorded. In *The Modern Jewish Canon,* to quote the title of Ruth R. Wisse's recent history of Jewish literature, female writers continue to remain in the margins. The fabric of contemporary Jewish women's writing is made of threads that date back to the very beginnings of this literature: to the Yiddish-language memoirs of Glückel von Hameln, née Pinkerle (1645–1724), chronicling the life of a businesswoman with thirteen children; to the conduct manuals for Jewish women by Judith Cohen Montefiore (1784–1862) advancing the radical idea that women should attend synagogue services; to the letters and novels by Rahel Varnhagen, Fanny Lewald, and Henriette Herz, the Jewish salonnières of Romantic Berlin, advocating women's rights, tolerance, and universal education. Writing at the beginning of the seventeenth century, the Italian Jewish poet Debora Ascarelli may very well have been the first published Jewish woman writer, while Rachel Luzzato Morpurgo (1790–1871) usually is considered the "first female modern Hebrew poet" (Baskin, 23).

The tradition of Jewish women's writing in the Diaspora and in Israel is difficult to reconstruct in its entirety because it encompasses vastly different historical, national, and societal contexts and languages. There is room for more research and discoveries, and there certainly is room for a figure like Michelene Wandor's minstrel Isabella; after all, one does not simply inherit traditions—one changes them by appropriating them, and one reinvents them if they do not appear to yield what one is looking for. The insight that "cultures, as well as identities, are con-

stantly being remade" (Boyarin and Boyarin, 721) also pertains
to traditions.

The repertoire of themes, motifs, narrative strategies, and
genres employed by contemporary Jewish women writers, however, is rooted in the literary production of their predecessors,
which in its beginnings favored autobiographical genres such as
diaries, memoirs, and letters. The essays of Myriam Anissimov
("A Yiddish Writer Who Writes in French") and Barbara Honigmann ("On My Great-Grandfather, My Grandfather, My Father,
and Me"), both included in our anthology, are autobiographical
self-portraits of the young artists as daughters and granddaugh-
ters. Anissimov claims a certain history of Jewish writing (writing in Yiddish) as a project that she would like to continue with
her own means (by writing in French). Honigmann critically re-
views a different history of Jewish accomplishments in the Diaspora to cancel the contract of acculturation signed by her forefathers. Like many a text authored by Honigmann and by her
colleagues, this piece, too, straddles the line between fictional
and essayistic writing. It also comments stylistically on a Jewish
cultural past in which the world of the *sefer* (book) was inhabited
more or less exclusively by men, while women had to confine the
scope of their writing to the private realm of family life.

Large-scale family tableaux spanning many generations con-
stitute another genre, as seen in the work of Katja Behrens, Sarah
Frydman, or Nine Moati. But there is also a tendency toward
smaller vignettes depicting the personal hardship endured by
Jewish women set subtly against the backdrop of larger historical events. Here, too, contemporary Jewish women's writing is
in dialogue with women's literature at large as it emerged in the
1970s and 1980s. The stories in this volume by Marlène Amar
("On the Edge of the World"), Ludmila Ulitskaya ("March
1953"), and Reina Roffé ("Exotic Birds") all sketch responses to
events that imperil the biographies of their protagonists. Carl
Friedman, on the other hand, juxtaposes two diametrically op-
posed forms of contemporary Jewish identity in her story "Holy
Fire": the female narrator who was disowned by her Orthodox

family for her nonconformist attitudes reckons with the funda-
mentalist turn of her friend's son, who becomes a militant Zionist. But only on the surface does Friedman's story comment exclusively on the male politics of fundamentalism that lead a
pious father to disown his daughter and a young man from the
Dutch provinces to kill Palestinians. The story also juxtaposes
two different ways of reading the great Jewish texts—that is, of
relating to the Jewish tradition: while the male militant seeks
encouragement in literal readings of the scripture ("Wasn't it
written in black and white?"), the female narrator finds pleasure
in the "sound of the language and the metaphors" of the Torah
and in the figurative language of Kafka.

To be sure, our anthology can provide only a small segment of
this rich literature. Our selection of authors is based on choices
that were not always easy ones; without any constraints of space,
we could have represented, in addition to the writers mentioned
in this introduction, Jessica Durlacher from the Netherlands,
Susanne Levine from Sweden, Pia Tafdrup from Denmark, or the
German-language writer Gila Lustiger from France.

   Also, by no means do we claim to offer an exhaustive survey of
the stylistic repertoire of contemporary Jewish writing in the new
Europe. Our decision to include only unabbreviated narratives
does not represent a penchant for a certain genre. Rather, it reflects
our consideration for readers who deserve to be told a good story,
as well as our desire to offer a selection representative of the prevalent features characterizing present-day Jewish women's writing.
We unfortunately have had to leave out poetry and thus could not
include, for example, any poems by Zsófia Balla from Hungary.

We have grouped the texts according to four overriding themes:
displacement, reemergence, defiance, and reinvention. "Displacement" explores how women are responding psychologically
and physically to their geographical and cultural dislocation.
"Reemergence" conveys the ways in which anti-Semitism af-

fected and permanently transformed Jewish life both at the personal and the communal levels. "Defiance" captures the determination to stand up against anti-Semitism as well as against Jewish fundamentalism. "Reinvention" reclaims displacement, reemergence, and defiance as the source of creativity and the impetus for playful, yet painful, confrontation.

The reader may keep in mind that the aims of this anthology are modest ones: we simply want to offer a handshake across the Atlantic, introducing authors whose work stands up to the comparison with the literary accomplishments of their fellow women writers in the United States, in Latin America, and, last but not least, in Israel. The editors hope that, following this first encounter between these European writers and readers outside of Europe, there will be more to come.

Notes

1. This symposium took place at Wellesley College (Massachusetts) in April 1999 and was followed by another one in Stockholm in February 2002, hosted by the European Institute for Jewish Studies (Paideia). Both events were organized by the editors. Unless otherwise noted, the statements by the authors used in the following biographical sketches are taken from the program notes and were prepared by the writers themselves.

2. Marlène Amar, in her statement prepared for the Wellesley symposium.

Works Cited

Amar, Marlène. *La femme sans tête.* Paris: Gallimard, 1993.

Anissimov, Myriam. *Sa Majesté la mort.* Paris: Seuil, 1999.

Baskin, Judith R. "Women of the Word: An Introduction." In *Jewish Women in Historical Perspective,* edited by Ruth R. Baskin, 17–34. Detroit: Wayne State University Press, 1998.

Bernard, Catherine A. "Anne Frank: The Cultivation of the Inspirational Victim." In *Experience and Expression: Women, the Nazis, and the Holo-*

caust, edited by Elizabeth Baer and Myrna Goldenberg, 201–29. Detroit: Wayne State University Press, 2003.

Boyarin, Daniel, and Jonathan Boyarin. "Diaspora: Generation and the Ground of Jewish Identity." *Critical Inquiry* 19, no. 4 (1993): 693–725.

Cixous, Hélène. "Mon algériance." *Les inrockuptibles* (August 20–September 3, 1997): 71–74. Translated by Eric Prenowitz as "My Algeriance: In Other Words, to Depart Not to Arrive from Algeria." *TriQuarterly* 100 (fall 1997): 259–79.

Clifford, James. "Diasporas." *Cultural Anthropology* 9, no. 3 (1994).

Delamarre, Alexandre J.-L. "Méditation sur la modernité." *Esprit* 29 (1979): 80–96.

Hartman, Geoffrey H. "On the Jewish Imagination." *Prooftexts* 5 (1985): 201–20.

Honigmann, Barbara. *Eine Liebe aus Nichts.* Berlin: Rowohlt, 1991.

Jabès, Edmond. "This Is the Desert: Nothing Strikes Root Here." In *Routes of Wandering: Nomadism, Journeys, and Transitions in Contemporary Israeli Art,* edited by Sarit Shapira, 246–56. Jerusalem: Israel Museum, 1991.

Klüger, Ruth. *Still Alive: A Holocaust Girlhood Remembered.* New York: Feminist Press at the City University of New York, 2001.

Ozick, Cynthia. "Toward a New Yiddish." In *Art and Ardor,* 149–77. New York: Knopf, 1983.

Showalter, Elaine. "Feminist Criticism in the Wilderness." In *The New Feminist Criticism,* edited by Elaine Showalter, 243–71. New York: Pantheon, 1985.

Steiner, George. "Our Homeland, the Text." *Salmagundi* 66 (1985): 4–26.

Szita-Morris, Eva. "Hungary: Relighting the Flame." *European Judaism* 23, no.1 (1998): 55–59.

Wandor, Michelene. "Voices Are Wild." In *Women's Writing: Challenge to Theory,* edited by Moira Monteith, 72–89. New York: St. Martin's, 1986.

———. *Gardens of Eden Revisited.* Nottingham: Fire Leaves Publications, 1999.

Wasserstein, Bernard. *Vanishing Diaspora: The Jews in Europe since 1945.* Cambridge: Harvard University Press, 1996.

Wisse, Ruth R. *The Modern Jewish Canon: A Journey through Language and Culture.* New York: Free Press, 2000.

Voices of the Diaspora

DISPLACEMENT

On the Edge of the World

Marlène Amar

Marlène Amar was born in 1949 in Colomb-Béchar, a place she calls "a small town lost deep in the Algerian Sahara." She says of her family: "My father was in business. His ancestors came from the Draa's mountains in Morocco. They were nomads and jewelers by profession. My mother belongs to the Jewish aristocracy. Her family was composed of princes, Maecenas, and other erudite people." During Algeria's war for independence, Amar and her family moved to Paris. She received her doctorate in French literature from the Université de Nanterre and, after working as a teacher, became a journalist. She now writes as a film critic for Le Nouvel Observateur. *Her first novel,* La femme sans tête (The Woman without a Head) *appeared in 1993, followed by* Des gens infréquantables (Bad Company) *in 1996 and* Princesse ma chienne (Princess My Dog) *in 1998.*

Amar reflects on her attitude toward writing: "When I write, I don't think of myself as a woman, or as a writer, or as Jewish. I am of course all of those simultaneously, and at the same time, before my sheet of paper, I am nothing. Or a kind of antediluvian creature who came from nowhere. Literature has nothing to do with militancy. One can only tell stories, even if these stories sometimes serve to rouse consciences. But to tell them, I believe one must be as free as possible, even in the way in which one defines or perceives oneself." She maintains that "Europe after the Holocaust is not so different from Europe before it. One still sees the same nationalistic rages, the anti-Semitism, an unchanged racism."

✽

Every day at siesta time, when under the scorching heat of the
sun the little town of Kenadza was breathing its last, Madame
Karsenty would settle down on the sofa in the living room where
her son, Theophile, was dozing and rub his head. Having done
the noontime dishes, Fortune, her daughter, would sit down at
their feet facing them with a book open on her lap. Under the
movement of the caresses, her brother's chest gradually began to
sag, his arms would unfold and fall gently alongside his body,
and as the muscles slackened in his face, it began to glow with
an expression of pure bliss. Next to him, her fingers fussing with
her hair, chin raised, and staring into space, Madame Karsenty was
sighing, sounds lost in the silence of the surrounding desert. In
the filtered light of the closed shutters she resembled a Madonna,
with her haughty bearing, her fine smooth skin, her long and
delicate nose, her sensuous lips that showed just a slight bitter-
ness, and her wavy hairdo tied with a silk ribbon at the back of
her neck. Entranced by the vision of the gradual softening features of the one, the frozen beauty of the other, and the silent intimacy that bound them, it took Fortune every effort to concentrate on reading.

  She was only seven years old but already had an exceptional,
almost worrisome fondness for observation. When noticing her
presence, her mother pushed her aside with an imperceptible
motion of her leg, and she would leave to look at other things.
Everything was an object of interest to her: the people she came
across, the dunes where she would go for walks, the animals that
lived there, the print in a piece of fabric, the embroidery on a fez,
the facade of a house. The smallest stone could capture her attention for hours and hours. Then she wouldn't notice time passing or the day coming to an end. It was not unusual for her father,
after lowering the metal curtain of his hardware store and leaving for home, to find her crouching in the dark, absorbed in the
scrutiny of a column of red ants, of snail shells delicately chis-
eled by the wind, or of a gypsum flower.

"Come into the light," he would tell her as he readjusted the skullcap on his head, "you're going to ruin your eyes." And she'd go home with him, skipping happily in his wake.

The infinite variety of faces, in particular, never ceased to astound her. Whether it was handsome or ugly, square or oval shaped, whether it had vitality, grace or not, whether it breathed goodness or deceit, intelligence, stupidity, or foolishness, to Fortune each face was worthy of interest. She never grew tired of noticing the shape of a nose, the line of a mouth, the roundness of a forehead, the gentleness or the brassy sparkle of a look, the charm or the betrayal of a smile, the determination or the weakness of a profile, the bluish pallor of the delicate opalescence of rings under someone's eyes that moved her so. Sometimes she would try to envision the complicated bone structure beneath the flesh, the configuration of a skull, the design of a jaw; she would try to grasp the secrets and torments behind the masks, to guess the past from the curves in the lines of a face, the stories and legends inscribed there. Still, it seemed to her that, no matter what she did, she would never manage to penetrate the astonishing, unfathomable, and boundless mystery of faces! One day many years later, when she had become a saleswoman in a ladies' clothing shop in the Paris Opera district, the boss had taken her to task: "Miss, please stop staring at the customers!" But since she was unable to keep herself from doing so, despite her efforts, she had been fired.

What exactly did this fixation, this obsession with observation, correspond to? Was it her particularly dreamy nature? Was it a thirst to know what surrounded her? Was it alienation of some sort that would let her see only that which she wanted to see, canceling all the rest, in a kind of settlement, a tacit agreement with life? Or was it rather those little kicks from her mother that, by excluding her insidiously from the family circle, had by the same token sent her careening from the world, as if on the rebound, thereby predisposing her to observe it rather than to take part in it?

Even her own face was a source of interest to her. Not a day went by that she wouldn't stand before the hallway mirror devoting herself to a careful scrutiny of her own reflection. Physically, Fortune was a strange little girl with a dreamy look and a curious face. She had a huge head that always leaned toward her shoulder as if it were too heavy to be carried upright, a scrawny body, enormous black eyes, the pointy nose of a weasel with a beauty mark on its bridge that everyone took for a bit of dust and would try to wipe off, a mouth so thin that it got lost at the corners in the fold of her too plump cheeks, and short plain brown hair.

Whom did she resemble? Not her father, who had a coarse profile and the compact stoutness of his ancestors, mountain people of the Draa. Not her brother, who was the image of his father. Not her mother, either, who came from the Tafilalet and whose beauty had no equal. One day her aunt Aziza had shown her photographs of some ancestors who at the end of the nineteenth century were jewelers in the Erfoud region, and in them she discovered a familiar look, in the satiny texture of the skin, in the shy smile they revealed, in their expression both open and proud, and in the gaze of astonishment that enlarged their eyes. They always posed as a group in the pictures. The men stood in a half circle, their look piercing. They wore *jellabas,* loose embroidered pants, and fezzes stitched in gold in the Arab fashion. In majestic beauty, the women were seated in front of them, some with babies in their arms. Their complexion was smooth, their dark eyes outlined in black, and their features were harmonious and classically elegant. They carried themselves ceremoniously. They were sumptuously attired in long striped or flowered dresses with many layers of underskirts. Their foreheads, wrapped in bands of fabric, were adorned with unusual horn-shaped headdresses or covered with silk scarves knotted at the back of the neck from which hung heavy silver chains. They wore many necklaces and earrings with precious stones.

Fortune had wanted to know more about them, but her aunt was unable to satisfy her curiosity. Through the years and through the trials and tribulations of their eternal wandering all traces of them had been lost. Most of them had lived in the Jewish quarters of the cities they had come through and, as other Jews before them, had been reduced to the status of *dhimmis*—the inferior place in which the Sephardim were held—which kept them enslaved. There they were abused, mistreated, and had become victims of extortion. If they had not fled, they had perished, assassinated by the *kaids* who, under the authority of the sultan of Morocco, governed the province of the valley of the river Ziz. That was all Aziza had been able to tell her. Afterward, her niece had often asked to see the photos again, each time delighting in the imperial nobility that could be seen in their eyes, despite the bitter fate and humiliations to which they had been subjected.

Fortune knew nothing about the land of her ancestors, nor even about Algeria, her own country. She had never left the boundaries of the Kenadza district where she was born. Two years earlier her father had taken her to the zoo of Colomb-Béchar, seventeen kilometers away, to see the fennecs—small long-tailed and sharp-nosed foxlike animals—the hyenas, and the last lions of the Atlas Mountains. That was it. She knew nothing about the rest of the universe. She didn't even have an inkling life existed beyond the dunes. She had always had the gratifying feeling of being precisely where she was supposed to be. And yet nothing ever happened in this town lost in the middle of the desert. Except for an occasional accident in the coal mines or a cloud of grasshoppers that would destroy everything in its path, no event at all would occur to change the course of things. Beneath the white heat of the sun the streets were almost always deserted. The ochre houses, which barely eroded in the sandstorms, formed the shelter for muffled little lives that made no noise. Minds seemed submerged in never-ending indolence. The hours passed at such a crawl that one might have thought time had forgotten this unlikely spot on the map of the world. But this slow-paced existence, the faint breath of this somnolent society, the deep silence that reigned over everything suited Fortune very well. Childhood's minuscule moments of elation were enough for her. Eternity and the prevailing opposition to change were commingled for her. She expected nothing more than that the days would follow each other in the same way they had before, languid as always, with the same lapping human sounds and the same rituals. So every afternoon after school, when the air would become protectively cool, she went back to her old habits and would go off through the town abandoning herself to her inspections. She didn't have any specific goal. Here she'd find Tuaregs, their faces colored blue from their long indigo scarves, bargaining with Bénichou, the tailor, for a few remnants of fabric. There, crouching on the ground, children were playing jacks under the detached eye of a couple of old men sitting in the doorway of their house, intent on eating sunflower seeds. Elsewhere still, on the terrace of the Café Loti, the anisette drinkers had taken up their post to stare at the well-balanced behinds of the laundresses returning from the wadi or at the wrapped silhouettes of the Muslim women coming out of the Turkish baths. Farther along, the clergy from the surrounding hovels were going through the streets praying, their heavy eyelids opening and closing at the rhythm of their chanting like sails billowing in the wind.

Fortune was still enveloped in the haze of childhood, where everything is amorphous, in which objects, other people, and feelings are the constant in a blur of consciousness developing. She did not suspect that all these scenes, these faces, these colors, these different impressions would inspire the paintings she was to create later on. But she already had a vague sense that these observations and these persistent strolls on the edge of the world were bringing her supreme pleasure.

The immutable unfolding of the hours gave Kenadza the appearance of a wax theater. Every morning, the sun would rise over an immovable setting, over unchanged actors who seemed to be interpreting the same role as the day before, going to the same places, meeting the same people, sitting on the same chairs, making the same gestures, pronouncing the same words with the same invariable expression of ashen vacuity in their eyes. The eternal repeated beginning of this suspended spectacle suited Fortune's lethargic nature. She liked nothing better than this daily rendezvous with a familiar world that never moved.

Still, some evenings a celebration would take place and shake up the fine order of this endlessly peaceful performance. A wedding, a bar mitzvah, or the birth of a boy—always welcomed as a gift from heaven, in contrast to that of a girl—everything became a pretext to come together. From the predinner drink hour on, the air was laden with unaccustomed animation. People would dress up and find each other all along the main street. The news of the day was exchanged, grandmothers' remedies against a scorpion sting or a high fever were swapped, and the recent visit of the ministerial representative was discussed. Then they would come together at someone's house around long tables bedecked with casseroles of *dafina*—a stew of vegetables and meat—salad bowls full of white mushrooms, dishes of couscous, chicken, baby lamb, and little meatballs. The appetites were stimulated with glasses full of anisette, old records were taken out, and the evening went on in an incessant commotion of children's cries, ululations, and oriental chants. While the women were busy serving and clearing, the men would stuff themselves, empty bottles of whiskey and date liquor like water, make jokes, sing at the top of their lungs, hesitantly follow some dance step—alone or in pairs—to old music, and then, unsteady on their feet, they would leave to get some fresh air in town.

Fortune didn't like the emptiness their eyes reflected at those moments, the irises that would become lost in the whiteness of their gaze, the overly relaxed bodies, the incoherent phrases, and the tempestuous laughter that would shake them at times and make them look like madmen. That is when she would go and sit in the dunes on the other side of the wadi. And beneath the bright moon and the stars frozen in the sky, in the sweetness of the night and the silence, disturbed only by the flight of a group of wild ibises in the distance, the barking of a dog, or the burst of the drunken voices, the most radiant part of herself reveled in the celestial beauty of the desert, as in a dream.

TRANSLATED FROM THE FRENCH
BY MARJOLIJN DE JAGER

Exotic Birds

Reina Roffé

Reina Roffé was born in Buenos Aires in 1951 and immigrated to Spain in 1988, where she has been living in Madrid. At age seventeen, she wrote her first novel, for which she received the Pondal Rios Prize for best young author. Among her novels are La rompiente *(1987),* Monte de Venus (Mount Venus, *1976), and* El Cielo Dividido (The Divided Heaven, *1996). Her collection of poems* Silogismo en falso (Syllogism in Error, *1982) and many of her stories have been translated into English. She is the recipient of many literary prizes and honors.*

In her most recent novels, Roffé explores a sense of "inner and outer exile" as well as "the journey from our Jewish origins in search of our mythical lost paradise. Writing emerges from the ancestral memory." She elaborates: "Despite their different origins, authors who include elements of exodus, diaspora, and emigration in their fictional and poetic works are voicing problems of the Diaspora that have been felt and utilized for centuries by authors of Jewish background. These experiences and themes — like initial memories — represent the raw material for our literature. They are rooted in our childhood and nurtured primarily by the stories transmitted to us by our grandparents and parents, those who raised us." In her own work, Roffé has looked back to her Sephardic grandmother, who was born in Spanish Morocco and who immigrated to Argentina at the beginning of the twentieth century. Her purpose in doing so was to reconnect with this part of her grandmother's family history and to trace its path: "Evoking her in my writings implied a reevaluation of the peninsular Spanish language, the language of storytellers

*and of those who recite romances; my grandparents' Spanish was spat-
tered with Hebrew, Greek, and Arabic words acquired in their lands of
banishment."*

*

During the bitterest days of my European exile, I turn to the
photo album where I keep, along with more recent memories, a
few images from my childhood—images that, enlarged and corrected, come back to me in dreams and in disturbing moments
of insomnia. That is when I see the child I was and the people I
loved and when my first and perhaps only home comes clearly
into view. In that house, as if onstage or in a boxing ring, everyone defended his or her own territory with blood, sweat, and
tears. Aunt Reche, however, seemed to stay behind the scenes:
she didn't want to fight over the space; she wanted to leave it. I
secretly shared her desire. We both believed that beyond the
walls of that house a kind of salvation awaited us.

Aunt Reche waited for several years, passing up many inci-
dents that would have given her more than enough reason to
leave, until she finally found the right opportunity. One never
knows when a dead branch will sprout flowers. In fact, I never
did find out how that particular argument started in the kitchen,
the epicenter of daily quarrels. I am convinced that it was nothing serious, because only a few words and shouts were exchanged,
but it was the drop that made the glass overflow.

I remember watching a bird trying to fly across the patio in
the oblique drizzle that had been falling since morning when I
heard a clear, forceful voice.

"I'm leaving for good."

After making the announcement, Aunt Reche ran through
the hallway heading toward the stairs.

She was finally running from the house and from herself. What
was she like? What had she been like just moments before some
alien power took over and put her in motion? That motion was

now suspended in its own impulse, in the fury of escaping, in her legs, her feet, her step, in the slight sway of her entire body.

She was a tired woman. Her tiredness was not new; it was as much a part of her as was her pale skin, her slight smile, and the eyes that revealed her disgust, her tedium, the smothered cry, and the conviction that nothing was worthwhile.

When she was little, she used to walk along the dirt streets of a pretentiously named town in the province of Santa Fe until she reached the train station, where she would hide and dream of getting on that train that would take her to Buenos Aires. However, when the family finally did move to the capital, she was interested only in the port where the Sephardic Jews from Morocco used to disembark, among them her own young parents, who arrived at the beginning of the century.

As I remember her, I find it difficult to attribute her permanent air of melancholy to her nomadic appearance (she always seemed to be somewhere else). None of the stories about her provides a reason to justify her absence, the withdrawal into herself that made her invisible to everyone else.

No one ever saw her. Her apprenticeship for becoming invisible must have started very early, when she was still a child and spent long hours following the paths of the ants along the cracks in the flagstones. There must have been something in her infancy, in the solitude of her childhood days. But in her case, it was a different kind of solitude, one without which nothing was possible for her.

In the Jobson-Vera mansion, where she was born around 1925, her parents and siblings ignored her, not because they didn't love her but because of her determination to be ignored, to become a colorless spot, an imperceptible filigree on the floor or on the walls. The teachers used to give her very high grades in school, but they complained that she was like an extension of the bench she occupied in the classroom: dull, quiet, doing what was required.

She was compliant. I know she was especially dedicated to the

Friday afternoon chore she assumed when she still lived in the small town. Lacking a synagogue, the Sephardic community of Jobson, consisting of three or four families at that time, had improvised a prayer room in the back room of the store that belonged to her father, the grandfather that I never met. Seldom did the ten men needed for the rabbi to begin the ceremony appear. Aunt Reche had the job of going in search of those who were missing. She didn't understand this law, but although I can imagine her indignation at the fact that women's presence didn't count, I am convinced that she took her weekly duty very seriously. According to her older sister, who never kept secrets for her, once when Aunt Reche couldn't find the tenth man, she decided to take his place. She put on the cast-off clothes of the men of the house, covered her blossoming curves with a large coat, greased down her hair, put on a yarmulke, and took her place next to the other men.

She went unnoticed on that occasion and also again at the age of twenty when she repeated the feat, needlessly, in the temple on Piedras Street in Buenos Aires, no less, which was always full. These are the only mischievous things or transgressions she is known to have committed. Later on she lost interest in everything and decided to act like a robot whose actions were preprogrammed.

And in spite of that, her heart beat quickly. Even today I believe I can hear her rapid, furious puffing on the day she ran toward the stairs with the intention of reaching the last door of the house. I have her image frozen in my memory: Aunt Reche moving against the cobalt blue background; Aunt Reche who felt emotions, who felt love and anger although she was submerged in death. Certainly she expected more than anyone else did. How much more? A little more affection, a little more tolerance, the little extra promised by the lottery, the illusory bonuses of the business of life? I suspect that the magnitude of what she hoped for had become a burden, all out of proportion to what she could bear.

From there, perhaps, came her sleepless nights and the premature knowledge of failure and sorrow—a primordial, preexisting, unyielding sorrow that nevertheless made her rebel against her own knowledge that life was only life passing by. Could her relentless, barren insomnia have been the cause of these impressions? How could she fill the void, flirt with the darkness without going crazy with the thought—first innocent and then obsessive—that all effort was in vain, that love was a meaningless fiction, nothing more than an etcetera that justified all the theories that popular philosophy at once proposed and rejected in sayings, proverbs, songs, and movies. The only real connection for her was the ticktock of the clocks, the predictable church bells, the emergency sirens, the catfight on the roof, the pulse of the night pounding in her head.

Her silence also added to her invisibility. Words left her mouth with great difficulty. She pronounced them one by one in a low voice, with resistance and with a savage blush on her pale cheeks that made people very uncomfortable. For Aunt Reche words must have sounded worn out before being spoken, trivial and unnecessary. She didn't say words, she threatened to say them; in truth, they became entangled on the tip of her tongue and turned against her in an interior mumble.

The few people who could see and hear her felt more than a platonic veneration toward her. There were never any rumors about her being in love or having a lover; she maintained her virginity intact.

In my memory and in the photos Aunt Reche seems as attractive as most of the girls of her time and social class. What's more, between the age of twenty and thirty she radiated a surprising charm that made her stand out from the prettiest girls. Perhaps in the subtlety of her ways and in her depths there was a dissuasive touch that intimidated the men, that impeded their approach, that dissolved their initiative. Those who might have wanted her quickly exchanged desire for respect.

It was a respect she probably longed for in a different order of things: in her everyday negotiations, in the most immediate reality that, to her dismay, was hostile and dull. Everything affected her, leaving its mark on her like a whiplash: the ferocity of her mother, who called her a piece of meat, the domineering men of the house, her sisters' selfishness, the neighbors' stupidity, the intolerance of certain members of the community. She didn't cry because she knew it was useless, but she acknowledged receipt with a tangible desperation. If someone had extended a hand toward her, they would have felt the tense net in which she was wrapped.

I can imagine, based on my own experience, that it was in the darkest hours, the hours of insomnia and lucidity, that all the pieces joined together to form the jungle where the trees were flames and the beasts were screeching as if it were the end of the world. And so the day's smallest discomfort became a sharp pain. By the time night had ended, all of this anguish had left her empty, unable to share her feelings with anyone. She was uninhabited but not dead, and that was her worst defeat.

There was a time when she did want to live like everyone else. They say that she looked for a job, begged her parents to let her work outside of the home. They permitted it; she was already twenty-five, and they knew that she would be an old maid. I can imagine her on the bus, watching tired people blissfully dozing in their seats. How she would have loved to change places with the fat woman whose nostrils quivered from her heavy breathing as her energy yielded to the deep, refreshing sleep that would allow her to wake up smiling like a baby.

A pat on the shoulder, followed by a kind of envy of the lightness with which others went through life, would awaken in her the need for intense physical activity. They say that she would often walk thirty blocks to work. In the office she did her own work and that of two or three colleagues. She ate in the noisiest bars so that the chatter, the exuberant gestures and voices, the simple, spontaneous happiness flowing from the other customers would stick to her bones and break her silence. The noise enlivened her, made her eardrums tingle, her bones vibrate, her tongue click, her teeth chatter until she exploded within, mute, more alone, more abandoned than before. Some days she would end up exhausted. But she slept little; three hours was a major accomplishment. And the following morning she would be doubly tired—from her natural fatigue and from the extra physical exhaustion—thus becoming even more of a phantom figure.

There was no solution. An unfailing inversion of values was at work in her. Every project she took on in an attempt to be like other people went in the opposite direction, went astray. I am sure that with time she learned to laugh at herself, which perhaps afforded her the only intimate satisfaction that she was capable of fully enjoying. Although she was able to enjoy her own personality, which her family had declared incurable, her comings and goings began to assume the self-assurance of a saint. Rather than a transformation, it was the full deployment of the dominant traits of her temperament. Her calm manners, so habitual in her, became static. Her naturally white complexion took on a porcelain look. She seemed sculpted in marble or plaster or, more precisely, glass. Because of this transparency, she truly looked like an image carved in crystal, through which other bodies were visible in the light, as if she were an open window. When someone looked and spoke to her, they didn't address her but rather the person behind her.

On one occasion—Aunt Reche told me this herself—she saw her younger sister in the street and, believing she was waving at her, responded by waving back, but her sister walked by without recognizing her to meet someone else. This episode made her laugh to herself, a laugh she swallowed like a bittersweet morsel. The fact that she was still invisible at the age of forty, even when she did not want to be, tasted like a liberating elixir on the one hand (she could pass by imperceptibly like a fly's eyelash and laugh at everyone), but on the other hand, it was like the aftertaste of poison that had made her insignificant, like a flash that disappears at the speed of death.

Death? She showed some sparks of life at times, although they only lasted as long as a falling star. Because that day, when her mother again told her that she was nothing but a piece of meat, and Aunt Reche answered that she was leaving for good, her en-

tire body shook with a flourishing vehemence. She ran through
the hallway toward the stairs, a crucial area of the house where
all the profound arguments and the most violent rejoicing took
place. At that instant the steps that led to the street, as I remember them, stood out from the rest of the house like a re-
deeming space of arrival and departure.

It was raining, and near the back of the house a bird was flying over the patio. Aunt Reche had reached the foyer and then
the first step without losing her courage. I was trying to push her
along for her sake and for my own. But she needed to catch her
breath on the landing. This brief pause before opening the screen
door and going down to the main door stopped her, stopped her
definitively.

Perhaps during that decisive moment of hesitation it occurred
to her that it was better to stay with her own than to risk living
among strangers. The familiar solitude had a tone less desolate
than the solitude of exile. Or maybe she thought that it really
didn't matter where and with whom she lived: a woman who resides only in her private world is a stranger for everyone, everywhere.

As she retraced her steps, Aunt Reche was still trembling, but
she possessed the serenity of a surrender to her own battle, as if
she had accepted a verdict, as if she had had a revelation. Her
look was that of a game warden surveying exotic birds.

TRANSLATED FROM THE SPANISH

BY MARGARET STANTON

REEMERGENCE

Beyond the Bridges

Ruth Beckermann

Ruth Beckermann was born in 1952 in Vienna, Austria, where she studied art history and journalism. She has written and edited several books on the Jewish past and presence in Austria, among them Die Mazzesinsel (Matzoh Island, *1984*) *and* Unzugehörig: Österreicher und Juden nach 1945 (Not Belonging: Austrians and Jews after 1945, *1989*). *Her documentary films include* Wien Retour (Vienna Retour, *1983*), Die papierene Brücke (The Bridge Made of Paper, *1987*), Nach Jerusalem (Toward Jerusalem, *1991*), Jenseits des Krieges (East of War, *1996*), *and* Homemad(e) (*2001*).

Reflecting on the situation of Jews in Austria in the immediate postwar era, Beckermann states: "In Austria, Jews were permitted to live again after 1945 if they behaved and kept their mouths shut. To be sure, as the first chancellor Figl emphasized, Jews were permitted to practice their religion, but he warned them not to demand any compensation or privileges, otherwise there might be a new kind of anti-Semitism. Their special fate under the Nazis was posthumously taken away from them. Jews were not needed politically in the Second Republic. The representative role that they played in West Germany as a sign of new democracy was given to the political resisters" (Ruth Beckermann, "The Glory of Austrian Resistance and the Forgotten Jews," in Insiders and Outsiders: Jewish and Gentile Culture in Germany and Austria, *ed. Dagmar C. G. Lorenz and Gabriele Weinberger {Detroit: Wayne State University Press, 1994}, 251–59).*

*

The river invites no one to cross it. Neither the Danube with its
artificial island nor the Danube Canal. The latter, still an unreg-
ulated arm of the river, was a factor in the founding of the Roman city of Vindobona. To this day it is located in the center and
at the same time on the margins.

I spent my childhood years on this side of the canal. I do not remember ever having walked across into the Second District. We
took the streetcar for excursions to the Prater and the Danube
beaches, otherwise there was no reason to cross over the bridges. On
the contrary, without knowing what had actually happened there,
we were afraid of that miserable part of town that smelled of war.

We did not know that roughly one-third of the approximately
180,000 Viennese Jews had lived in the Second District of Vienna, that on November 9, 1938, five synagogues had gone up
in flames and thirty prayer houses been destroyed. We, the children of survivors, knew nothing at all. In conversations with
Jews born after World War II in Vienna, you can frequently hear
statements like "My childhood was spent in a no-man's-land" or
"We did and did not live here."

These memories do not capture the truth, although they do
describe a perception of the truth. We lived in a provisional Vienna, a place where we socialized almost exclusively with Jews
and talked about our imminent departure. It was as if, in the
midst of Austria in the 1950s, we were acculturated to the image
of a distant Austria, one that emerged in the literature of yester-
year and had nothing to do with the immediate past and present. Until the 1980s we discussed our experiences and observations discreetly and only with our closest friends. Even the word
"Jew" was taboo. We were students of the "Mosaic faith," staring at the crucifix where our supposed victim languished, a
crucifix that hangs on the wall of every classroom to this day.

But let us go across the bridges.

Let us take along an old photograph of that part of town from
the time Joseph Roth, Elias Canetti, Manès Sperber, and many

others described so aptly. You can see the Schweden Bridge. And there, where insurance and bank buildings tower over the city today, the photograph shows the two large coffeehouses—Fetzer and Stierböck. From the Danube Canal well into the Prater, coffeehouses covered this entire district, which is popularly referred to as Mazzesinsel (Matzoh Island) because it was both an island and the most Jewish district of Vienna. These coffeehouses were less elegant than the famous literary and social spots in the inner city, but they fulfilled many functions. Business was conducted here; people played Tarock and chess and read all the papers of the monarchy. Here political assemblies were held and, on the Jewish high holy days, prayer meetings. One such coffeehouse on Tabor Street was called the American Spot. At this place, unemployed people and potential emigrants could obtain information about the "country of unlimited possibilities," addresses, and immigration law. After the pogrom of November 1938, many people saved valuable months of desperate searching because they knew these facts and could find badly needed asylum.

The fact that not one genuine old coffeehouse can be found in today's Leopoldstadt speaks louder than words. After 1938 the coffeehouses had to close one by one because the world of which they had been a vital part began to vanish, along with their predominantly Jewish clientele. Today McDonald's tries to imitate the elegance of a substitute coffeehouse with the help of chairs à la Thonet. There are other attempts to adapt this district to the nearby city. However, the sweeping broom of those eager to embellish the city is not really effective, and the Second District remains less bourgeois than the other nine districts inside the outer belt.

It feels good to step out of the city, which has come to resemble an extension of the petty bourgeois living room. As a tourist favorite, Vienna is loaded with nostalgic public telephone booths, rustic benches, tacky streetlights, and potted plants. Already the "bunglers" have worked their way across the Danube Canal, where a Johann Strauß-Schiffscafé (Riverboat Café) and a flea market have been established to lure Viennese and visitors alike.

At the present time blueprints are being developed for the homey decoration and efficient use of the canal banks.

Despite the fact that two or three fashionable restaurants have already opened, offering "nouvelle Viennese cuisine" as their specialty, the district still belongs to the underground "milieu" after sundown. This is the time of day when shady figures emerge that the Nazis were unable to eliminate as thoroughly as the Jews through their cleansing: vagrants, smugglers, whores, and pimps. They crowd the espresso bars, wine halls, and the hotels that rent their rooms by the hour, as well as the red-light district for child prostitutes behind Venedigerau. Mexico Square, close to the Danube River, is the center of cigarette smuggling and illicit trade in all kinds of goods. This is the meeting place of Central Europe. The Poles have become the object of the populist anger, raging not only in the "golden Viennese hearts" but also in those of most other Eastern Europeans. It hardly comes as a surprise that, albeit by only one point of a percent, even in this traditionally "red" district, Jörg Haider's supposedly "Liberal Party" defeated the Socialists for the first time, using as its slogan for the 1990 election "Vienna Must Not Become Chicago." This victory occurred despite the fact that the predominantly Socialist government (paradoxically after the fall of the Iron Curtain) had passed a visa requirement for Polish citizens entering Austria and even encouraged the Austrian military to hunt for illegal immigrants at the supposedly open Hungarian border. It appears that a small country like Austria can get away with activities for which Germany was criticized, for example, sending weapons to Iraq (Austrian distributors were in third place) or making visas for Poles mandatory.

Despite all this, Leopoldstadt continues to attract foreigners. Since the 1970s even Jews began to arrive. The majority came from different parts of the Soviet Union and some from Israel. The Lubavitch Hassids opened day care centers and schools for new immigrants of whom the local Jewish communities were suspicious for a long time. By now, the approximately six thousand members of the overaged community have begun to consider the positive aspects of the population increase, and the newly opened Jewish middle school in the Second District now accepts Russian children. In the Tempelgasse, where the largest synagogue of Vienna used to be located, a Sephardic Center, including an apartment building and a prayer house, is being constructed.

Jewish people are no longer hiding. The massive onslaught of anti-Semitism caused by the Waldheim affair proved that even in the "city without Jews," ethnic prejudice continues to survive. Jews have recognized that prudence and assimilation were not in their best interest. During that time the illusionary nature of the compromises they had made became clear. In order to live in Vienna, they had to accept conditions that demanded they repress their own history, make a new start, and act as if that were, in fact, possible.

In order to legitimate their existence in Austria, the Jews themselves bought into the popular stereotypes of the "evil German" and the "roly-poly" Austrian. They managed to cope by projecting fanciful images of a Jewish-Austrian symbiosis into the past, glorifying an era of only one lifetime (1867–1938, the time during which Jews had been citizens and endowed with equal rights). In retrospect both parties of the "symbiosis" were fashioned into equal partners who gave life to psychoanalysis and modern music in an exemplary cooperative effort. What is forgotten is that the Jews achieved their accomplishments despite the pettiness of their Viennese environment and against its resistance. One forgets that the Jews conducted a "one-sided dialogue," trying in every imaginable way to make themselves understood. But who except for the anti-Semites answered them? What Gershom Scholem said about the German Jewish symbiosis is equally true for Austria. He termed such a symbiosis a myth because a dialogue needs two people "who listen to one another, who are ready to see the other person for what he is and what he represents and to respond to him."[1]

The longing for a symbiosis brought about great works of art by severing actual experience from the desired image that was supposed to remain intact. Contradictory emotions had to exist side by side because their fusion would have shattered the tenuous identity. Bitter and painful anti-Semitic experiences had to be repressed time and again and considered a private matter, while those signs that reinforced the desired image were underscored. However, the Viennese Jews have become more skeptical and recognize the shabbiness of a city administration that tried to compensate for the loss of face incurred during the Waldheim debacle by offering charity toward its "Jewish fellow citizens," granting a little money to establish a Jewish vocational school in two dilapidated rooms close to the Praterstern and a Jewish museum in a building completely unsuited for the purpose.

Despite its "new" Jews, the streets of Leopoldstadt do not lend themselves to imagining the former character of this part of town. The Leopoldstadt of the prewar era must have been unique, very different from the rest of Vienna, and at the same time it was so much a part of the city that it did not seem exotic. This is why hardly anyone considered it worthwhile to describe and photograph it during the time of its existence. Only after normal communal life had been destroyed and its particular atmosphere was lost did it become an object of contemplation. For example, Sigmund Freud, Theodor Herzl, Alfred Polgar, and Arnold Schönberg grew up here, but they never discussed this district as a phenomenon, because they did not consider it one. The Leopoldstadt of the 1920s was a phenomenon only for someone who was passing through, like Joseph Roth.

At the time, a Jewish rhythm of life influenced the district just as much as the Christian rhythm. Not only different religions but also different social classes lived here side by side—the population of Leopoldstadt could not be forced sociologically or ethnically into the corset of uniformity. The principle was diversity. It was possible, for example, to be a Jewish Socialist, a Communist, a Hassid at one of the "courts" that had moved from Eastern Europe to Vienna during World War I, a member of the small Sephardic community, or a Zionist. Some people were Zionists and at the same time adherents of social democracy;

others considered themselves assimilated Viennese Jews, distancing themselves form Eastern European Jewry; yet others abandoned their Jewish religion or did not even remember that they were Jews at all. By the 1920s the Jews had become a multilevel community. Some were more committed to their affiliation with a class, a profession, or a political group than to their Jewishness. This astonishing development had taken place within one or two generations. Only after the revolution of 1848 had the Jews been allowed to move freely within the Habsburg monarchy, to settle in Vienna, and to conduct different trades. Vienna became a magnet for the Jews in Bohemia, Moravia, Hungary, and Galicia. The new northern railroad carried thousands of them into the capital city. While the Jewish bourgeoisie moved into the formidable residences of Praterstraße, Jewish craftsmen, merchants, and workers mingled with the native population in the side streets.

"In those days Leopoldstadt was still a fashionable and distinguished district," Arthur Schnitzler reminisced about his childhood in the 1860s. "And the main thoroughfare, on which the Carl Theater stood, managed to preserve some of its festiveness even during the quieter hours when an elegant and carefree world came tearing back from the races or flower shows in their equipages and fiacres. During my childhood I often enjoyed the exciting sight from the windows of my grandparents' apartment."[2]

At that time the representational great Jewish temples were erected in the vicinity of this luxurious and vivacious Praterstraße. Industrialists, major businessmen, and intellectuals, despite all their professed liberalism and enlightenment, had them built to promote their own glory rather than that of the Lord. At the corner of Rotensterngasse, their Christian counterpart was built—the Johannes von Nepomuk Church, now gray and worn like everything else in this district today. During the turn-of-the-century *Gründerzeit,* when representation and religion went hand in hand, it was the Sunday meeting place. Nearby two large synagogues were erected in conformity with the predominantly ornamental piety of liberalism—seeing and being seen were a higher social obligation.

On the right-hand side of Praterstraße was the Großer Temple (Great Temple). Earlier than the architecture of the Ringstraße (Ring Boulevard) and even more vividly than the nearby Nepomuk Church, its Arabic motifs expressed how the extravagant but confused, intellectually repressed but economically expanding Viennese upper middle class wished to represent itself. On the left side of Praterstraße one could find the "Turkish Temple" as the complement and counterpart of the Ashkenasic Great Temple. It was an octagonal miracle of pseudo-Ottoman architecture, imitating patterns of the Alhambra. However, there were also other synagogues in Leopoldstadt where Viennese Jews attempted to reconcile their traditional spirituality with their newly gained status as "genuine Austrians"—the Polish Temple and the Emperor Franz Joseph Memorial Temple (Kaiser Franz Joseph-Huldigungstempel). Aside from these buildings there was the Schiffschul, the synagogue of the Orthodox Hungarian Jews. At the time of the Republic all these places, including more than thirty prayer houses of the most pious and the poor, were the ceremonial centers of their respective communities. All of them were destroyed during a single November night in 1938.

There were already visible danger signals after World War I when Vienna had changed from the cosmopolitan center of a multination empire into the oversized capital of a starving republic. At the very place where the tradition of integrating other groups and individuals was upheld, Karl Lueger's anti-Semitism grew into a mass movement and foreigners became the object of hatred. At precisely the same time, approximately 350,000 people were moving westward in an unprecedented flow of refugees. At the end of the war roughly 25,000 Jews from Poland remained in Vienna, most of them in Leopoldstadt, where they found cheap places to live and formed a social network. Perhaps half of the 120 Jewish associations after the war were charitable associations. For example, there was the Verein zur Bekleidung und Unterstützung alter Männer israelitischer Konfession (Association for the Clothing and Support of Old Men of Israeli Faith) and the Verein zur Unterstützung armer Talmudschüler (Association for the Support of Poor Talmud Students).

Joseph Roth wrote about the Eastern Jews living in Vienna in the 1920s: "The Leopoldstadt is a voluntary ghetto. Many bridges connect it with the other districts of the city. During the daytime, merchants, peddlers, stock-exchange brokers, businessmen, in other words all the unproductive elements of the Eastern European Jewish immigration, cross over the bridges. But in the early morning hours also the progeny of the selfsame unproductive elements cross over these bridges; the sons and daughters of the merchants who work in the factories, offices, banks, press agencies, and industrial workshops. The sons and daughters of the Eastern Jews are productive. With their parents' barter and peddle, their children are the most talented lawyers, doctors, bankers, journalists, and actors."[3]

In the interwar period they contributed to the unique ambiance of "Red Vienna" as the most enthusiastic adherents of the intellectual and messianic Austro-Marxist movement, which (like psychoanalysis and Zionism) had evolved at the time of a specifically Viennese Jewish identity crisis of the fin de siècle. The radical changes of the year 1918 had led to a departure from the old. The hoped-for result was a new epoch that could be conquered through human labor and technology. To this day the erect, muscular statues of this period with their broad chests and their hollow spines stand everywhere in the midst of a decor symbolizing technology, streamlining, and faith in progress. Also the Jewish youth of that time, even if they dreamed of socialism or Palestine, possessed an optimism that in retrospect seems incomprehensible.

But not everything then was as delightful as it is made to appear to this day in the euphoric recollections of many who witnessed those years. The Eastern Jews were the first targets of the anti-Semites, who tested their weapons on them. As early as 1919 anti-Semites armed with canes promenaded along the bridges of the Danube Canal and were an everyday phenomenon. In the course of one of their spectacular forays in December 1929, Nazi hoodlums devastated the elegant Café Produktenbörse on

Taborstraße because it had the reputation of being a "Jewish" coffeehouse. Three years later, at the Jewish New Year's celebration, they ravaged Café Sperl, where a temporary prayer house had been established. They battered the praying people with metal sheaves and demolished the furniture. The photographs of Jews on their knees who had to scrub the streets with toothbrushes after the invasion of Austria, euphemistically referred to as *Anschluss* (annexation), were seen all over the world. They document the end of Matzoh Island.

   After my stroll through the Second District, I have arrived in the Große Schiffgasse, once again close to the bridges across the Danube Canal. On summer evenings the singsong of Jews at prayer emanates from the open windows of an apartment. Every once in a while someone looks down on the large empty space between buildings covered with vegetation growing wild—it was here that the synagogue, the Schiffschul, used to stand. It continues to be a monument of extermination. The history of this gap has not yet been marked by one of the little plates with the red-and-white Austrian flag that are used to explain historic sites all over Vienna. This gap is as transitory as the memory of the victims. Already it is covered with grass. Soon a new house will take its place.

TRANSLATED FROM THE GERMAN

BY DAGMAR C. G. LORENZ

Notes

   1. Gershom Scholem, "Vom Mythos deutsch-jüdischer Symbiose," *Judaica* 2 (Frankfurt: Suhrkamp, 1970), 7.
   2. Arthur Schnitzler, *My Youth in Vienna,* trans. Catherine Hutter (New York: Holt, Rinehart and Winston, 1970), 14.
   3. Joseph Roth, *Juden auf der Wanderschaft: Wien,* vol. 3 of *Werke in drei Bänden* (Cologne: Kiepenheuer and Witsch, 1956), 657.

A Yiddish Writer Who Writes in French

Myriam Anissimov

Myriam Anissimov was born in 1943 to Polish parents in a refugee camp in Sierre, Switzerland. After the war, they settled in Lyon, France, where her father, a self-taught author of works in Yiddish, established himself as a tailor. Anissimov studied philosophy, photography, and acting. In 1966 she moved to Paris to establish herself as an actress, a singer, and eventually a writer. She changed her name when her record producer told her the name Frydman was too Jewish; she picked Anissimov at random from the telephone directory.

Anissimov comments on her relationship to France and its culture: "The Western world, and particularly France, participated in the killing of the Jews — thus I could only feel a deep hostility toward this {French} foreign culture that was imposed on me. But at the same time, I had to know it and to appreciate its qualities. I took from French culture the intellectual tools that were necessary for me to develop further what I had received from the world of my parents."

Her first novel, Comment va Rachel? *appeared in 1973, followed by eight more novels, most recently* Sa Majesté la mort *(His Majesty, Death, 1999). She also is the author of two biographies, one of Primo Levi* (Primo Levi: La tragédie d'un optimiste, 1996, *translated as* Primo Levi: Tragedy of an Optimist) *and one of the French Jewish writer Romain Gary* (Romain Gary: Le caméléon, 2004). *Her works are widely translated, and she has received many awards, among them the Ordre des Arts et Lettres awarded by the French Ministry of Culture.*

33

Anissimov sees her writing as a form of commemoration: "Everything I write is dedicated to the Judaism that disappeared in the ashes and in the graves of the Shoah. It is to this vanished world that I am tied and to which I pay homage. These dead ones, they are my family. I remember them every moment of my life."

*

I belong to that peculiar generation of Jews who have the duty to speak Yiddish, my mother tongue, in a tongue at once familiar and "foreign"—French. Though Yiddish is still used as a vernacular language by the Hasidim, primarily in New York, Meah Shearim, and Bnei Brak, it is about to disappear outside of these purely religious groups. But Yiddish—"Jewish speech"—was spoken by ten million people fifty years ago. In Eastern Europe, the Jewish civilization conceived of the world in Yiddish, that language born of fusion on the banks of the Rhine in a hostile environment.

Before the catastrophe, the *Hurban,* hundreds of Yiddish newspapers appeared daily, and writers imagined modernity in an idiom that the Germans considered an offense, a spit into the face of the great Goethe.

Yiddish vanished in the ghettos, in the massive graves that the *Einsatzgruppen* made the victims dig before massacring them; it vanished in the gas chambers of the extermination camps. The dead exchanged their last words in Yiddish. In front of the cheerful murderers, mothers pacified their children, they bid them farewell in Yiddish before they were thrown with them into the hole full of men, women, children, and blood. Children separated from their parents in the "sewer" of Treblinka howled *"Mamele! Tateh!"* It is this reality that has occupied my consciousness ever since I was four years old, when a bloated young man, the brother of my father and a survivor of Auschwitz, came to our house. He recounted the miracle of his survival and the murder of his entire family, of our entire family, of a entire people in Yiddish, which had become the language of the dead. The photographs that showed heaps of cadavers had inscriptions in Hebrew letters. It was in Yiddish that my father told me not to forget them: *Farges nicht!* (Do not forget!).

Yiddish, to my childish eyes, had become an idiom which only we understood and which marked our horrible peculiarity: that of a group destined to die which had—legitimately? I asked myself—survived.

Every year in the spring, on a Sunday morning we would take a walk along a small path on the edge of a forest. We did this in commemoration of the execution of Châtillon d'Azergues. Jews who had been rounded up in the streets of Lyons had been slaughtered in this forest. Everything was peaceful when we arrived. I saw some flags at the beginning of the procession. One heard only the songs of birds and the sound of our footsteps on the pavement. All of a sudden, the mother of a fifteen-year-old boy who had been one of the victims started to weep and to yell in Yiddish. Others came up to support her while the hymn of the Vilna Partisans gradually drowned out her voice: "*Zog nit kein mol az du geist dem leztn veg*" (Never say that you are walking the last road).

The Yiddish writers who had survived addressed only a handful of other survivors. We, the naturalized Jewish children, were considered by the state as future citizens practicing the Mosaic faith. Nothing of the sort! My father, devoted to the Enlightenment, a former Bundist, a member of the UJRE (Union of Jews for Resistance and Mutual Aid), did not set foot into the shul, not even on Yom Kippur—though that did not prevent him from waiting on the sidewalk for his sister, smoking a Boyard rolled in corn paper. But on Yom Kippur he did not work and lit candles to commemorate his parents. Yom Kippur was still the dead. But the living? Sunday mornings, on Place des Terreaux, my father debated endlessly in Yiddish, and in the afternoons in the library of my grandfather over a glass of tea.

Nowadays, Yiddish libraries are frequented by melancholic Jews capable only of stumbling through a few sentences with a lot of effort, their minds inundated with short-lived images. But there is not only the sound of Yiddish, there is also the "smell" of Yiddish. To me, the smell of the Eastern European Jewish dishes is closely linked to the sound of the Yiddish language. And there is not only the smell of the kitchen but also of the Workshop. I write "Workshop" with a capital letter because the Workshop was a whole world. The strange country in which I grew up and which no longer exists. The huge room where the sewing machines were humming, where steam rose, releasing the fabric finish under the ironing cloth and the weight of the gas iron pushed by the presser, and where scissors cut dryly through the padding of coats along marks of chalk.

I cannot hear Yiddish spoken without having an immense feeling that is never accompanied by a feeling of joy. My dreams are situated around the snatches of Yiddish, and my broken memory is a dark abyss full of ashes. A few rare photographs show us the catastrophe taking place. Fleeting images in black and white that show naked women carrying their children in their arms in front of the entrance to the gas chamber, executions, naked bodies thrown into the trench.

Other images, in color, taken by the Nazi Walter Genewein in the Lodz Ghetto (*Litzmannstadt, die Stadt der Zukunft*—Litzmannstadt, the city of the future—for the Nazis) and sold to an antique dealer in Salzburg in 1957, tell us how the Jews lived in the antechamber of death. Chaïm Rumkowski, the chairman of the *Judenrat,* had prophesied: *"Unzer einziger weg is arbeit"* (Our only way—of survival—is work).

Primo Levi tells of a Polish Jew arriving at Auschwitz who, astounded to see that he spoke Italian, reprimanded him: "If you don't speak Yiddish, you are not a Jew." Was it to convince himself of his Jewishness that Levi, agnostic that he was, forty years later devoted a year to learning to read the major language spoken in the extermination camps? Thus, Levi, the Enlightenment intellectual, joined the enormous crowd of those who had been swallowed up; commemorating them, he learned a few essentials of their language and wrote a book (*Im lo akhshav mataï* [*If Not Now, When?*], based on a Hebrew saying from Rabbi Hillel)[1] in order to immortalize a part of what had been annihilated.

The books that I have written have their source in the sparks, the phrases, the words of the Yiddish language. As poor, faulty, and miserable as they may be, these Yiddish sources have taken on considerable importance. So impressive that they now hold up, fuse themselves into the structure of French, which is only the support, the vehicle of a feeling born in another world. They are strengthened by other materials from a vast, imaginary structure: the charred walls of the houses in the shtetls, the walls of the ghettos, the walls of the synagogues, the pale walls of the gas chambers, Yiddish. Every word of the Yiddish language is familiar to me, but it lies in me as if at the bottom of a grave, where one exhumes the fragments of bones by rifling through the earth.

It was in this state of mind that I, as an unknowing child, had to learn to read and write French. It was not an easy task. My teachers reproached me for seasoning my written French with neologisms that were both foreign and horrible. "Are your parents French?" one teacher commented.

Those disgraced words, crossed out by red lines, were fragments from conversations heard in the Workshop, because we also lived in the Workshop. I had to remove them from the territory of my papers, full of remorse and resentment. I am proud of having reintroduced them into the hybrid language of my books. It is without a doubt on this fertile ground of the conflict between French and Yiddish that my own manner of writing— may one call it style?—developed. Nothing had been premeditated. I had made no decision, had not created a theory, to achieve this result.

If the Yiddish world that vanished in the Shoah belongs to the land of myth, of fantasy, I have kept alive in me the voice of my father and of my grandfather, of my aunt Souralé, of my mother. I still have the miraculous privilege of being able to hear Yiddish spoken in Paris, to recognize the savory French mixed with Yiddish that animated Paul Morand when he, in search of strong feelings, ventured through the narrow streets of the Marais.

The thousands of books in Paris's Medem Library will have no more readers when the last Yiddish-speaking Jews have dis-

appeared. The millions of volumes printed in Yiddish everywhere in the world will no longer be in demand, no longer held
or read. Those who wrote them will be forgotten, except for the
few privileged ones who had been translated. At best they will
become objects of scholarship. This abyss that we feel inside us
will grow even wider. Then silence will come. Yiddish will no
longer be heard. Authors will no longer be fertilized by its music,
its humor, its sensuality, its poetry. Yiddish will have the status
of a dead language, but for some of us—types who are also disappearing—it will be like an amputated limb whose sensory
memory remains intact. We will have definitively lost the world
of our origins.

My mother bestowed upon me my grandfather's six hundred
books. I draw strength to write in French from contemplating
time and again their canvas jackets, deciphering with a kind of
a shudder the letters of the Hebrew alphabet in works that were
printed in Lodz, in Vilna, in Warsaw, in Paris, in Buenos Aires,
in New York, and in Moscow, before and after the *Hurban.* To my
amazement, I hear, close to the Yiddish flickering in the shadow
like the flame of a candle, sentences coming out in French. They
preserve, regardless of the circumstances, a link to the demolished world of my origins. Thus, permanently linked to a language marked by the sign of destruction and death, I became "a
Yiddish writer in French."

TRANSLATED FROM THE FRENCH

BY THOMAS NOLDEN

Note

1. This meditation of Rabbi Hillel the Elder is taken from *Pirkei Avot*
(*Sayings of the Father*) 1:14: "*Im ein ani li mi li? / Ou Keshe ani leatzi ma ani?
Ve im lo akhshav mataï?*" (If I am not for myself, who will be for me? / If I
am for myself, who am I? And if not now, when?).

Jews

Clara Sereni

Clara Sereni was born in Rome in 1946. Her first book, Sigma Epsilon, *was published in 1974. After working for several years in politics and as a translator of Balzac, Stendhal, and Madame de Lafayette, she returned to writing in 1987 with the publication of her second book,* Casalinghitudine (Housewifeliness, *translated into English in 2002). This was followed by* Manicomio primavera (Springtime Asylum, *1989),* Eppure (Yet, *1995),* Taccuino di un'ultimista (The Notebook of a Meek Woman, *1998), and* Passami il Sale (Pass Me the Salt, *2002).*

Sereni lives in Perugia, where she served as deputy mayor from 1995 through 1997. Taccuino di un'ultimista *recounts her memories from that term in office. Politics and personal experience also intersect in her 1993 book* Il gioco dei regni (The Game of Reigns). *In this documentary novel, she explores her own family's shrouded history: her uncle was Enzo Sereni, a key pioneer of Italian Zionism. Enzo was killed in Dachau in 1944, but Clara's father, himself a Communist and prominent anti-Fascist, had never been forthcoming in sharing this part of the family's legacy with his daughter.*

She says about her writing: "If I were to say what my objective is when I write, I would say that it is this: change the world, improve it. I believe this is the deeply Jewish element of my writing: a 'must be' which turns into a 'must do in order to change,' something I maintain is also typically feminine. I believe there is yet another complicated element which makes my writing deeply Jewish: the absence of the fresco-style approach, or a big picture. These are replaced in my writing by a mosaic style of composition, which is attentive to inquiry, to the meaningfulness of the single tassel, and to the connections between them rather than to any claim to give univocal and exhaustive answers. This is a way of writing which certainly has something to do with Midrashic speculation rather than with the Christian or Catholic tradition."

✳

Up until then she had never had any friends. Her mother's pronouncement ("That's the way she is," she would say) had the effect of making the two resemble each other, sheltering the girl from any effort or compromise: the kids' games were too rough for her, or too stupid, or caused her heart to beat so violently that it upset her. Her family didn't like the courtyard either with its mix of habits and words. Right from the first years of her life the dangers of the street and the world had been made present to her in the most uncertain of terms, as well as the need to camouflage herself in order to get ahead, to progress on that path of small satisfactions on which her family had embarked. She had become studious, reliable: somewhat sad, earnest said her mother.

The first day of high school the girls were swarming around outside the school: the voices of those who knew each other flew around; the others chatted loudly, immediately forming relationships and common interests.

Waiting to go in she remained silent, concentrating on the entrance door that was about to open. With her hand she gave an extra shine to her black school smock, then her hair, staring at the toes of her shoes to check that they were gleaming.

Once inside there was the same noise, voices and shuffling about. Then, in the classroom, in line, silence. The register, the names read out one after the other, at the same time she was told where to sit, in order of height or according to other ideas that the teacher had in her head. She looked at the other girls whose names were called out and feared for her tranquillity, for the order of things and thought. The hardly repressed unruliness of one girl scared her, as did the rude gaze of another; the stylish hair-style of a third made her feel embarrassed.

The desk she was given—toward the back on account of her height—was still empty. She put her book bag away and waited, with trepidation.

The girl who sat next to her was about as tall as she was, her hair tied in black braids that were neither too stringy nor too thick, her hands bore well-tended nails and showed signs of having done household chores.

The one was almost a copy of the other, and this gave the girl's beating heart some relief. After school, not knowing who to say good-bye to, she chose her new classmate, calling her by her sur-name, as one did at school:

"Bye, Zarfati," she said softly, and the girl answered with a great sweep of her arms and said, "See you tomorrow."

Getting used to her new surroundings was less difficult for her than on other occasions. Zarfati did not dig her in the ribs to show her mistakes and anomalies that she didn't want to see, she didn't leave crumbs on the desk from her snacks, and all in all did not produce any surprise or embarrassment. Out of habit she continued to shield the answers she wrote to class exercises with her hand, preventing anyone from copying. At the same time she began to feel a measure of curiosity and to stare more and more at her schoolmate, becoming familiar with her face, her gestures, her way of dressing.

From the indiscreet chatter of playtime she found out that Zarfati's parents had a drapery shop, which explained the lace she wore on her collar and that pink ribbon in her hair, of the kind her mother had not been able to buy for her. The worn-out and shabby overcoats both girls wore told of the long history each one had: but the fashionable buttons on Zarfati's gave it a shine, and she was jealous of this.

At the end of the first term Zarfati received an average school report, but hers was mediocre: keeping a low profile, being one of the crowd was no longer enough. School now required proof of confidence and enterprise for which she was hardly prepared.

Initially they had praised her for her discipline and silence, but now in gym class they demanded she have the straight back she had never had and that she shout out so loudly with the other girls that she got a sore throat. The whiteness of her blouses did not protect her from negative comments, which had serious repercussions on her school report. It was for this reason that her mother went to talk with her teachers and came home upset by the charges of feebleness leveled at her daughter and by the suggestion that she encourage her to study with others and so become more open and self-confident.

She thought of Zarfati, for there was no one else she could think of. Yet the idea of seeing her afternoons invaded, of the competition between her clothes no longer protected and rendered inoffensive by the black school smock, and of the two girls' bodies scared her. Under her blouse her bust was beginning to grow; it embarrassed her and the extra intimacy could perhaps destroy the silence that guaranteed her peace.

Doubts, anxiety, fears. She studied more energetically to prove that she could do it on her own. At the gatherings of the Young Italians she forced herself to shout and from the swollen veins of her neck her voice finally found its way out. As if liberated, from then on, even with her mother, she abandoned whispering, accustoming herself to the stentorian tone that was then considered appropriate.

But soon came the time when she was quizzed in front of the class. She was as if struck dumb in front of the blackboard, the class expectant for the unanswered questions hanging in the air, ready to strike anyone who, sitting at their desks, felt they were safe.

The teacher, ever more impatient, repeated the question: but her head was empty, the thread of her argument lost, and the fear of the bad grade that was on its way made for even more confusion and prevented her from excuses and trickery.

Cutting things short, the teacher got up from her desk and wrote the answer herself on the blackboard. As she did so, for an instant, she turned her back on the class. At that moment, Zarfati signaled something to her with her hand, mouthed a silent word, and the answer was there, ready to be used.

When she went back to her desk, with the passing grade she had been given at the last moment, she was afraid she would have to repay debts of gratitude, requests that she would have to satisfy. She sat next to Zarfati without looking at her, out of embarrassment. And in the next class, during a class exercise, she still shielded her work against copying. Only after handing it in, and with the courage that came with an answer that was almost certainly correct, she decided, during recess, to say thanks to Zarfati.

"What for?" she answered. "Are we or are we not friends?"

Before that she had never thought that theirs could be called a friendship. The word brought her a warmth inside that lasted more than a day.

Her mother, worried that they would fail her daughter or force her to resit her exams in October, reprimanded her for the next school report, which was still mediocre despite her efforts. There was no talk of extra classes; it was already an effort to get her to study. Maybe she should find a schoolmate who was cleverer than she was with whom to do homework and go over the lessons. That was the only possible way forward.

She invited Zarfati to her house to study. Her mother prepared a snack for both of them before clearing up the kitchen and leaving them alone so they could concentrate. Thanks to a tip or two from her friend, the homework was over quickly without too much bother. They asked each other questions to go over what they had studied and in a little while the task was over, the solitary and heavy toil of each day now done with a minimum of effort, with some pleasure even.

Her grades improved rapidly; the afternoons spent together became a habit. Zarfati always came to her house, freer and more courageous in her movements than she was. She preferred it that way; she wasn't curious and to feel her nest behind her gave her the confidence to take a risk or two on the new terrain of the friendship that was her new adventure.

Now after homework they spoke of other things too. Zarfati suggested a new haircut, something inexpensive to brighten up the eternal gray overcoat, an ingenious way of putting on perfume. She learned to accept the gift of Zarfati's cleverness and no longer envied her buttons, nor even her grades, which were always better than hers.

They still used each other's surname when they talked, as a guarantee of the reserve that was still a part of their friendship. At the same time each felt the desire to be like each other, and their differences faded, dimmed. The big and loud world that surrounded them remained beyond the territory of the complicity and secrets in which they moved: their task was to grow; they didn't think they had to be bothered with anything else.

At school it began to be said that they looked like each other, that they were "the twins." They responded to the jokes and the fun that was poked at them with knowing winks, proud of their afternoons and their intimacy.

When school was over and the summer lay before them, Zarfati put forward an idea or two, but faced with her hesitations she didn't insist and they agreed they would see each other again at the beginning of the school year.

During the first empty, hot, and dusty days, she thought a great deal about her friend, as if she were a habit that had been abandoned. However, the return to the solitude, the silence of the kitchen she no longer shared was also the source of a strange ease, of a return to the mirror she liked, of put-aside disappointments: Zarfati, she knew, would be helping her parents in their shop, with no time for chatting and plans.

The summer was slow—this had never happened to her before. For the first time she envied the girls in the courtyard, recklessly racing and playing together, even when it was humid outside. One day (softly—where had that sure tone gone?) she asked her mother if she could go down and play too: the answer, "You don't really want to mix with those girls, do you?" was irrevocable, and she was even ashamed of the thought.

From the window with the blinds half closed she looked out

at the street, people, strangers, until her mother called her to do some household chore, or some sewing, which they did together. Devoid of joy, devoid of interest, she learned her mother's skills, which had now become old and useless to her eyes.

She missed Zarfati: perhaps if she had had her address she would have taken the risk. In the mirror, as she washed in the morning, she monitored her growing bust, the growth of her pubic hair, her rounder hips: in the absence of Zarfati's eyes she didn't know what to think, asking herself in the meantime if her friend had changed as much as she had, and how, and if they would still be friends.

When they met again the first day of school, their confidence was intact: again they called them the twins, again they studied together.

Then Zarfati didn't come to school, nor to her house to do homework: one day, two, many. When she came back, she had a serious air about her that made her seem older. Even her braids seemed stiffer, and the absence of ribbons made her seem gloomy. Cautiously, she asked if it was an illness or something else; the other had difficulty in answering. In the end, Zarfati spoke vaguely and in an embarrassed way of articles in the newspapers, laws, politics, her parents' concerns: distant things, difficult, which she thought could not have anything to do with their friendship.

No, she couldn't think that. For this reason, when she saw the fear in her friend's eyes, she encouraged her about the quiz in class and the school report, refusing any other worry.

A heavy silence fell over them, a distance whose causes she could not fathom at all.

They were in class; the teacher was about to arrive. Zarfati tidied the books in her desk, then sat up, her knees close together, her arms behind the back as prescribed. She wet her mouth with her lips and took a deep breath in.

"Next Wednesday it's my birthday," she said, not looking at her. "Do you want to come to my house?"

What a show of trust and intimacy she had asked of her, to face the unknown. But there was that distance between them to be made up, at any cost.

"Yes." She had made the commitment, without even considering her mother's permission or the effort it cost her to leave her part of town. "Do you know where Via Arenula is?" Zarfati asked and began to explain how to get there. But the teacher came in, and rolling her hand Zarfati made a gesture to say "later," she would explain how to get there later.

During recess Zarfati wrote down her address on the last page of her exercise book, but a quiz was scheduled for the next class, and they used the time to go over their homework.

She spent the evenings and Sunday embroidering, a cross-stitched cotton jabot she wanted to give to Zarfati. In the meantime she imagined what her house was like, and the streets she would walk down to get there, and the great adventure of having a friend who likes you. She thought about what she would wear and how she would do her hair that day, using all the tricks she had learned from Zarfati and the skills she had developed during the summer she had spent in solitude.

She asked her mother if she could go and she agreed, asking her only that she not get in the way and that she behave well.

Monday, Zarfati was not at school, but she thought there was still time, and in the evening she continued with her embroidery. Tuesday morning, she asked her mother to iron what she had made and then to hide it so that Zarfati, when she came to do homework, wouldn't find the surprise.

But Zarfati didn't come to school, nor did she come for homework. She began to have doubts but told herself that her friend would not let her down like that.

The next day, during the first lesson, the place next to her desk was empty: yet, there was still the chance of meeting her at the end of the school day, and she hung on to that hope.

The teacher came in to the class, and as usual the students stood up to greet her. From her desk, instead of taking the register, the teacher called out to a student sitting in the back row—

Maurizi was her name, a real ass—and told her to sit next to her and that from now on she would sit at Zarfati's desk.

Impertinent as ever, Maurizi moved her school bag and asked: "So, Zarfati's not coming?"

The teacher lowered her eyes to look at the register, crossed out the name with a stroke of her pen, and said:

"No, she's not coming anymore. She'll go . . . she'll go to a more appropriate school. Or she'll get a job."

She accepted the betrayal without batting an eyelid, concerned not to give the other students any satisfaction.

She noticed some mumbling coming from the other desks, but order was immediately reestablished when their class work was handed out.

On the way out at the end of the day, she felt the threat of questions from the small groups of students who were hanging around near the school.

She said good-bye to them quickly and ran off before she could feel trapped.

In the following days she waited: she was expecting Zarfati to make up for the offense, the invitation to her birthday party, first made but then let drop. Sometimes she thought about going to the address Zarfati had hurriedly written down on the last page of her exercise book, but her part of town was a long way away, a street she didn't know. How could she venture out into that world without a guiding hand? Anyway, it had been Zarfati who had offended her with her silence, so it was up to her to make the first gesture toward reconciliation.

She didn't worry too much about what had happened to Zarfati; nothing could come between the trust that they had established. Yet, in their conversations no mention had been made of the plan to go to another school or to get a job: hence the betrayal, the offense.

Others disappeared from the school, teachers and students. With little fuss, and if comments were made, she managed not to hear them, consumed by a pain that was hers and hers alone.

And yet, there was something in the November air. Something that perturbed her, a suspicion of fear that accompanied her days and prevented her from studying.

With an excuse and not a little persuasion, she convinced her mother to take her to the part of town where Zarfati lived. Right there, near the Via Arenula.

Narrow, dark alleys, walls that pushed ever upward, suffocating whoever lived in those houses. The few passersby walked with lowered heads hugging the walls, hurriedly. The voice of a shopkeeper or two, someone calling out: even in the whispers you could make out a difference, incomprehensible, never-before-heard words.

A drapery shop. She understood that this was the place, and her heart almost missed a beat: from desire, from expectation.

Through the stained shop window, she saw Zarfati at work behind the counter.

The desire to run to her, to touch her, to speak. Her mother held her by her arm and said:

"Wait."

Zarfati came to the shop door: she was laughing, her braided hair slicing through the air, her hand held tightly in another girl's.

They sang, taking it in turns, Zarfati and that other girl:

—*Uno chi sapeva.*

—*Uno chi intendeva.*

—*Uno solo il creator.*

And then together in countermelody, the incomprehensible words:

—*Baruchù barushemà.*

Excluded, betrayed.

She did not have the strength to ask; she turned her back on the alleyway and on Zarfati.

Her mother was generous and avoided any comment.

"Let's go home," she said and gave her a brief and compassionate caress to say she was sorry.

To cancel out the waste and the memory, she used the embroidery she had done for a pillow to decorate the double bed, as well as the most beautiful doll she had been given as a baby: and the whole thing ended there.

But the pain didn't. Every time the thought came back to her, the wound was there, forever open with no hope of healing: in the absence of the medicine of words, time did not heal her but instead made the pain permanent.

In the days, months, and years that followed, she was always careful not to allow anything similar to happen to her again. From the adolescent that she was, she turned her attention to becoming an adult. She had a certain—but very limited—number of acquaintances, but she allowed none of them to become anything more.

A distrustful awareness always kept her sheltered from any risk. Soft colors were her choice: out of elegance, she would say, worried about too-strident contrasts. By her good fortune, life did not treat her too harshly: the bombings did not hit the house she lived in, the war did not take away from her either her mother or her father, who with some skill and a trip or two to the black market saw that she did not suffer the worst of hunger.

She thought it better not to get involved in the lives of others.

When she got married, her white veil was not very, very long, but her dowry still consisted of twelve pieces, as was expected. In church, when she said "I do," she rediscovered the strong clear voice she had learned at school.

Her husband always wore gray and was very down to earth, paving for himself a path to which she too made her contribution. She had two sons: the small passion she had inside her for lace and embroidery did not find expression with the two boys, but she was the kind of mother she was supposed to be.

When the first granddaughter was born, it was as if she herself had given birth, the enormous joy made her feel good, able to understand and to pardon: she allowed herself to love her daughter-in-law, even though she had changed her son.

Following the pediatrician's advice, she overcame the embarrassment that the public gardens, the sun, open and crowded spaces caused her. She got used to new methods, horse meat instead of a filet and fizzy drinks to cure stomachache. She accepted clothes that were different from what she had imagined. However, she made the jumpsuits look nicer and added little silk ribbons to the unisex sweaters.

The little girl attended a day care center and then kindergarten: on account of her son's and daughter-in-law's schedule, it was always she who picked up her granddaughter and took her home, she who tidied up her clothes and her life, she who took the stains out of the smock she wore to school, and she who dried her capricious tears.

In first grade, her granddaughter introduced her to her school friend, the one she shared a desk with, and asked if she could invite her for an afternoon snack.

She thought that the joy the granddaughter gave her was worth the risk.

On the day chosen for the visit, her house was tidier and cleaner than usual. She left the table ready: an embroidered tea napkin, glasses with flower designs for the drinks, bendy straws.

After school the little girls were very excited: she held their hands all the way home. She tried hard to think that a friend for her granddaughter could perhaps enrich her, another piece of life that was given to her.

When they took off their coats, she saw that the little girl was dressed soberly: a skirt with a tartan design, a little red cardigan; she glimpsed an embroidered ribbon on her blouse. She liked her calm movements, her thank-yous, which she said after any help was given, her reasonable and quiet demeanor.

Her granddaughter showed her friend the house, chatting with her about games and homework. From the kitchen, as she was preparing the snack, she heard their voices, their laughter, the happiness of being together.

She cut the little sandwiches, filled them with prosciutto ham; she took orangeade and Coca-Cola from the fridge, holding the cans tight between her hands so that they were not too cold: gestures of love for her granddaughter, and also for her friend, about whom she was beginning to feel happier.

She checked that everything was in order, then called the girls. They came into the kitchen, and her granddaughter immediately climbed up on the chair, starved. But the other little girl asked:

"May I wash my hands, please?"

She appreciated this as well and invited her granddaughter to follow her friend's example: the two little girls set off for the bathroom, then came back, their hands red from the exceptional care with which they had, evidently, scrubbed and dried them.

The two of them had a hungry look about them. Her granddaughter grabbed the sandwich and immediately sank her teeth into it. She poured the Coca-Cola or the orangeade into the glasses, according to who wanted what. The other girl picked up the sandwich, looked at it, and put it down on the plate: she gulped down the orangeade she had in the glass and then stopped.

She was worried about the little girl's tastes:

"Don't you like the ham?" she asked considerately.

"Oh no!" the little girl answered vivaciously, anxious not to displease her friend's grandmother, who had been so kind to her. "*A me mi piace tutto,*" she said. "I would ate anything. It's just that I'm not allowed to eat it."

"Why, because it makes you sick?" she asked, and in the meantime she put biscuits, a slice of cake, and cheese on the table.

"We don't eat ham; we're Jews."

A shudder of memory, a return to events from which she had taken her distance. The sudden and abysslike opening of a possibility, an explanation, a reason: the certainties and defenses of an entire life put into question by a single word: "Jews."

In a second, from that possibility, which she had never before been willing to consider, her life became confused, changing sense and meaning: the path she had followed lost its reason, and there began to grow in her a desire for lively, sunny colors—it was disturbing.

She put her hands on the marble countertop, anchoring herself to the certainties of always. She filled a glass with water and drank in little sips, slowly recovering the security of the strong, clear voice and of the choices she had made.

She poured out the Coca-Cola; she poured out the orangeade. She swept a few crumbs from the table.

The little girl took a slice of Parmesan cheese, ate it voraciously, and in the meantime looked at her to show that she was happy and did not want to disappoint her.

Her granddaughter started talking about school matters, and the two little girls wove a web of names, references, little secrets. When they began to create a magic circle around themselves, the kind that surrounds all children when they gather together, she could not allow it. With her refound voice, she said:

"When's your mother coming to pick you up?"

The little girl answered. Her granddaughter again called her back into the magic circle, but the grandmother didn't leave them alone anymore, and just as the circle was about to close again, she, with great care, broke it.

The little girl went away with her mother, who had come to get her: closing the door on their backs, her granddaughter said she was tired, carrying with her the disappointment of that strange afternoon, different from the way she had dreamt it.

She drew her to herself, put her on her knee, and cuddled her. There was something that the little girl couldn't understand; she should try to explain it to her.

"You know," she said, and her voice sounded wise, "it's not a question, but it's always best not to get involved."

"Who with?" said the little girl.

"With the people you don't know well; you never know who they are. Maybe you'll come across habits that are different from yours and you may not like them."

The little girl thought about those words, holding her finger in her mouth as she still did sometimes. Sweetly, her grandmother took her finger, massaged it, and held her hand in hers: gestures of comfort, gestures of love, familiar gestures.

"*A me il prosciutto mi piace.* I would ate ham all day long," said the little girl, as if she were concluding an argument on which she had been reflecting. "But I also like Parmesan cheese."

She sighed, sought out the words to tell her about Zarfati, the betrayal, the disappearance: her school friend's dark braids danced in front of her as if actually there.

She passed her hand over her forehead; she drove the image away.

"It's not 'I would ate,' it's 'I would eat,'" she corrected her granddaughter.

The little girl seemed as if she were about to make a puffing noise, but she avoided her impatience with a caress, a convincing one:

"The world is more complicated than you imagine it," she said, "and it's not as good."

Under the weight of that sentence the little girl was saddened, or maybe she was just tired: it was already late; soon her mother would come to take her home.

At the door, as they were saying their good-byes, grandmother and granddaughter made their usual arrangements for the next day after school: and if she wanted to bring some other schoolmate, she would not have anything against that.

Concerned to protect her from any disappointment and giving her a little tap on the cheek, the grandmother jokingly reminded her:

"And none of this nonsense about strange snacks, understand?"

TRANSLATED FROM THE ITALIAN

BY DAVID WARD

DEFIANCE

March 1953

Ludmila E. Ulitskaya

Ludmila E. Ulitskaya was born in Bashkiria, Siberia, in 1943. After studying biology at Moscow State University, Ulitskaya worked as a geneticist. She began writing only in the 1990s. Her first collection of stories was published in France because many of her screenplays, plays, and stories were subject to censorship. Among her novels are Medeya i ee deti (Medea and Her Children), *for which she received the French Medici Prize, and* Veselye pokhorony (The Funeral Party, 1999), *which has been translated into English and several other languages. Her most recent novel,* Kukotsky's Case, *was awarded the Russian Booker Prize in 2002.*

    Ulitskaya looks back to her childhood years growing up in a secular home: "I remember the last seder. It was conducted by my ninety-three-year-old great-grandfather in 1952 or 1953. Yiddish was his mother tongue; we spoke Russian." Ulitskaya has said that the Holocaust "stunned the world — Jewish as well as non-Jewish." She says: "The world was offered one more chapter of the Bible but it wasn't read. To my great sadness, the world didn't change after this shock. For new generations, this is an old story like the Great Flood, the massacre of children in Bethlehem, or St. Bartholomew's Night. Now we have Rwanda, Yugoslavia, and Chechnya."

It was an utterly dreadful winter, with the frost raw and suffocating, the clouds an especially dirty quilt which had slipped down on the hunched shoulders of a sunken sky. Great-grandfather had been bedridden since last autumn and was slowly dying on the narrow carpet-covered couch, looking round affectionately with sunken gray-yellow eyes and never unstrapping the phylactery with its scriptural texts from his left hand. With his right he held to his stomach a flat electric bed warmer enveloped in worn gray serge, the acme of technological progress at the turn of the century, which his son Alexander had brought from Vienna just before the Great War when he came back home as a young professor of medicine after eight years of studying abroad.

The bed warmer really ought not to have been allowed, but the mild mechanical heat alleviated his pain, and his oncologist son finally yielded to the old man's request and acquiesced. He had no illusions regarding the size of the tumor, the extent of the metastatic spreading, or the inoperability of the condition and deferred to the quiet courage of a father who in all his ninety years had never been known to feel sorry for himself.

Little Lily, his great-granddaughter, his favorite, with her shining brown eyes and her matte black hair, would come home in her brown school tunic, covered in chalk and violet ink stains, pink and loving, and would edge over onto the couch, on his sore side. All elbows and plump knees, she would pull the tartan rug over onto herself and whisper into his scrawny, hairy ear:

"Go on, Granddad. Tell me a story."

And Aaron would tell her of Daniel, or Gideon, of legendary heroes of the past and fair virgins, of wise men and czars with obscure names, all of them long-dead members of their tribe, until Lily was firmly persuaded that her great-grandfather, himself so ancient, must have known and personally remembered some of them at least.

It was a dreadful winter for Lily too. She too felt the special heaviness of the sky, the demoralization at home, the whiff of hostility in the streets. She was eleven years old. Her armpits ached and her nipples were revoltingly itchy. From time to time a wave of disgust would break over her at all the little changes taking place in her body, the swellings and the coarse dark hairs, the pustules on her forehead; her very soul protested blindly at all these disagreeable, impure things. Absolutely everything seemed revolting and reminded her of the greasy, carroty yellow film on the top of mushroom soup: dispiriting Gedike, whom she murdered daily on the cold piano, the scratchy woolen leggings she pulled on every morning, and the morbid violet covers of her exercise books. Only by snuggling up to her great-grandfather, who smelled of camphor and old paper, could she be delivered from the malaise that tormented her.

Lily's grandmother Bela Zinovievna was a skin specialist, and she too was a professor. She and Alexander were a sturdy pair who between them pulled no small load. He was a tall, bony man with large ears, given to cracking rather witless jokes, but with all his wits about him when performing in the operating theater. He liked to say that all his life he had been devoted to two ladies, Bela and medicine. Bela was plump and short, with penciled eyebrows and lips painted red; her hair was dazzlingly white, and she didn't give a fig for the competition's chances.

Both of them were curiously moved when they would come home from work to find the old man and the young girl lost in a world all their own. They would exchange a glance, and Bela would brush a tear from the corner of her eye, smudging the eyeliner. Her husband would drum his fingers on the table in warning, and Bela would raise an open hand, as if they communicated in deaf-and-dumb language. They had any number of such gestures, secret communications that left them with little need of words, divining everything as they did from the shared currents of their hearts.

Their aged father was taking his leave of life, as this sprightly couple recognized, and tarrying on the threshold of death, he was passing on some rather questionable wisdom to his posterity, a young girl on the threshold of puberty. The highly educated professors regarded these eons-old legends of an ancient people as a homespun garment that human thought had outgrown, unlike their own thinking, of course, disciplined and honed by the school of European positivism in Vienna and Zurich and trained to a scholarly athleticism. Worshiping only the cardboard god of nimble-footed scientific fact, they manfully lived their lives in comfortless but honest atheism. For all that, both of them felt that here on the threadbare couch, in the very presence of condescending Death, who was biding his time, a unique oasis was in bloom. Here there was no Jewish doctors' plot to poison the Politburo, and here the superstitious hysteria at the wickedness of the poisoners, which had possessed millions of people, had no dominion. Only here did the real poison—the fear, servility, and devil worship—retreat. Demoralized, living every day in the expectation of arrest, exile, or worse, the learned professors were reluctant to leave that dining room, a room shared by all in the house, where the old man lay ill, to pursue their scholarly routine. Instead they sat themselves in the armchairs beside that greatest, at the time, of all rarities, a television set (which was not, however, switched on), and listened entranced to the old man's cooing singsong. He was telling the tale of Mordecai and Haman.

They smiled to each other in an anguish of the spirit and made no mention of the lunacy into which they plunged each day on leaving home.

They had lived through a great war, had lost brothers, nephews, and numerous relatives, but they had not lost each other, their little family, or the full measure of their trust, friendship, and tenderness for each other. They had achieved a solidly based and unshowy success and should, it had seemed, have been able to count on a good ten years more, while health, strength, and worldly wisdom were in a happy equilibrium, to live as they had always wanted to, working through an all-too-busy week, going away at the weekends to their newly completed dacha to play Schubert duets on the rather indifferent piano they had there, bathe after lunch among the water lilies in the dark river, drink tea from the samovar on the wooden veranda in the slanting rays of the setting sun, and in the evening read Dickens or Mérimée and fall into sleep together in an embrace that in forty years and more had become so habitual that you couldn't tell whether its evident comfortableness came from an interlocking of their convexities and concavities however they lay, or whether over the years their nocturnal embrace had reshaped their bodies to the present unity.

They would already have had more than a fair share of distress in their lives from the long-standing conflict with their son, who had chosen of his own free will to work in an area into which no normal human being would have been lured at any price. He occupied an exalted but vague position, living in the frozen northeast beyond the Arctic Circle together with his bearlike wife, Shura, and their young son, Alexander. The gods seemed to be mocking them in the fact that the two members of the family furthest from each other should bear the same name.

In 1943 their son had brought his older child, Lily, to the military hospital in Viatka where his parents were working twelve hours a day at the operating table. The little girl was five months old, weighed seven pounds, and looked like a shriveled doll. From that day right through to the end of the war, they worked different hours, Alexander Aaronovich usually taking the night shift. Lily, restored to health and proper plumpness by Bela Zinovievna, stayed on with her grandmother and grandfather, reborn to the happy destiny of being the granddaughter of two professors at once. Knowing how ready her natural mother was to take offense, and Shura did on occasion come to see her, Lily's foster parents had her call them Bela and Alex. Great-grandfather she called Granddad.

Bela and Alex were sitting now in the old soft armchairs with their no-nonsense loose covers, half turned away from the couch, pretending they were not listening to what the old man and his great-granddaughter were whispering about.

"Oh, Granddad," Lily exclaimed in horror, "you mean to say they hanged absolutely all the enemies from a gallows?"

"I'm not saying one thing was good and another bad. I'm just telling you what happened," her great-grandfather answered, with a suggestion of regret in his voice.

"Other people will come to get even and kill Mordecai," the little girl said anxiously.

"Yes, of course," he said, cheering up for some reason. "Quite right. That's just what did happen. Other people came and killed those people, and then all over again. Let me tell you this, though. Israel lives not through victories: Israel lives because of . . ." He put his left hand with the phylactery to his forehead and extended the fingers upward. "Do you understand?"

"Because of God?" the girl asked.

"There now, I said you were a clever girl." Grandfather Aaron smiled his toothless, baby smile.

"Did you hear what he's filling the child's head with?" Bela asked her husband in vexation when they were alone in their bedroom, lying on what Alex laughingly called their double writing desk.

"Bela, my sweet, he's a simple shoemaker, my father, but it's not for me to lecture him. To tell the truth, I sometimes think I would have been better off a shoemaker myself," Alex said darkly.

"What way is that to talk! You don't get to regress!" dear, clever Bela responded testily.

"Then don't you go upsetting yourself on Lily's behalf," he smiled wickedly.

"Oh, you!" Bela dismissed him. She was a practical person, not given to ethereal speculation. "That doesn't worry me in the slightest. What does worry me, though, is that she will blurt something out at school!"

Alex shrugged. "My own dear Bela! That really doesn't matter any longer in the slightest."

***

Bela Zinovievna's fears were groundless. Lily had no chance to blurt anything out at school. Since last autumn, nobody in her class would talk to her. Nobody except Ninka Kniazeva, who the authorities kept meaning to send away to a school for mental defectives, only they could never get all the paperwork together. Large and bonny, Ninka had developed earlier than most girls from the north. She was the one girl in the class who, because she was feebleminded, was prepared not only to say hello to Lily but actually to be her partner when they were marching in a loud, shrieking crocodile to some museum that, invariably, had been awarded the Order of the Red Banner.

The times had generated their own rigid conventions: Tatars made friends with other Tatars, dunces befriended others similarly afflicted, the children of doctors played with the children of other doctors, and this was especially true of the children of Jewish doctors. Never in ancient India had the caste system been so risible and petty. Lily had been friendless since her neighbor and classmate Tania Kogan had been packed off by her parents to relatives in Riga before the New Year, with the result that the last two months had been insufferable.

Lily assumed every outburst of laughter or unwonted liveliness, every whisper was directed against her. Everywhere she went she heard them sneering and spitting out "Jew girl" at her, and most hurtful of all was the fact that she began to associate this gluey, resinous word with their surname, with Grandfather Aaron and his pungent leather books, the honeyed, cinnamon smell of the Orient, and the viscous golden light that always surrounded him and filled the whole of the left-hand side of the room where he lay.

To make matters worse, in some incomprehensible way, the two things enfolded each other and would do so for all time, the golden light that illuminated her home and that gluey, sneering spit word in the street.

Barely had the hoarse bell of freedom rattled out its long-awaited message before Lily had whisked her exemplary notebooks into her briefcase and was rushing on clumsy legs to the cloakroom in order to burst out into the fresh air as soon as could be, without time even to do up the buttons on her coat and the wretched hook at the neck. Then it was away over the lumpy, snow-gray, icy slush, through the puddles with their broken ice, her flipping and flopping galoshes splashing her stockings and the hem of her coat, one more courtyard to go, and into the stairwell of her block of flats with its reassuring smell of damp lime wash, then up the stairs to the first floor, gluey which didn't have a landing but only a smooth sweep of the stairs to the tall black door on which the welcoming brass plate with their awful, ridiculous, shaming surname, Jizhmorskii, was affixed.

Recently she had had a further trial to contend with. As she came out of the playground Victor Bodrov would be swinging on the great, rusty gate, waiting for her. Everybody was afraid of him, and he was known in the courtyards as Bodrik. He had blue, tinplate eyes and a face without features. The game was simple enough. There was only one way out of the playground: through Bodrik's gate. As Lily approached it, trying to burrow her way as deeply as possible into the crowd, her classmates, aware of what was to come, would either draw back a little or run on ahead. When she entered the danger zone, Bodrik would let her go forward a little before launching the gate with his foot. It would give a loathsome creak before crashing into her back. It did not hurt much, but it was humiliating. Each day the game acquired some new twist. One time Lily turned round to face the gate rather than be thumped in the back by it. She grabbed its iron rails and hung on.

Another time she stopped and waited a short way from the gate for a long time, pretending that going home was the last thing on her mind, but Bodrik was not short either of patience or spare time, and having kept her at bay for half an hour, he watched with satisfaction as she tried to squeeze through the railings of the school fence and failed. Even a skinny girl would have found it a tight fit, and Lily was further encumbered by her thick coat.

She scored a point on just one occasion by managing to skip through immediately in front of one of the teachers, elderly Antonina Vladimirovna, whose East Siberian face registered utter amazement at such bad manners.

The sport improved daily and attracted an ever-increasing crowd of spectators with time on their hands. Only yesterday they had been rewarded with the truly remarkable spectacle of Lily's desperate and almost successful attempt to climb over the flat, spearlike tops of the school's cast-iron railings. She first wedged her briefcase between two of the railings, then placed her foot in a place she had spotted earlier where some of the bars were bent. She had climbed right to the top, thrown one foot over then the other, only to realize her mistake in not having turned to face the fence. Rigid with fear, she maneuvered herself round and slithered slowly down, pressing her face against the rusty iron.

The hem of her coat caught on one of the spears. When she finally realized what was holding her back she gave it a good tug. The sturdy material, of what had been a professor's overcoat before being born again to made-over life covering her plump young body, stretched its uttermost, resisting with all its well-twilled fibers.

The observers hooted ecstatically. Lily flapped again like a great fat bird and, with a low ripping sound, the coat released her. When she reached the ground Bodrik was waiting, her muddied briefcase in his hands and a genial smile on his face:

"Good for you, Lily girl. What a gymnast! Want to do it again?"

And with the practiced hand of a huntsman tossing a decoy, he threw her briefcase up in the air, seemingly without effort, but in fact he flicked his wrist with the precision of an aborigine throwing a boomerang. The briefcase sailed upward, its sides bulging, turned over in midair, and fell back to the ground on the far side of the fence again. Everybody laughed.

Lily picked up her woolly hat with its two idiotic bobbles and, without a backward glance, using all her strength not to run, went off home.

Nobody chased after her. Half an hour later her friend Ninka brought her the briefcase, which she had wiped with a handkerchief, and pushed it through the door to her.

In the morning Lily tried hard to be ill, complaining of a sore throat. Bela Zinovievna took a quick look in her mouth, popped a thermometer under her armpit, glanced at the elusive column of mercury, and darkly pronounced sentence:

"Up you get, young lady. You've got work to do. We all have."

That was her religion, and she would not countenance the sacrilege of idleness. Lily crept unwillingly to school and sat out three lessons, oppressed by the prospect of her ineluctable passage through the gates of hell. In the fourth lesson, however, something happened.

The date was as yet only March 2, and the wheel of the unsinkable ship of the Soviet state had not yet slipped from the grasp of its Great Helmsman. Alexander Aaronovich and Bela Zinovievna, had they heard from their secretive granddaughter of this incredible act of courage, would have been very heartened.

Toward the end of Lily's fourth class Antonina Vladimirovna, with a glint from the most animate part of her face, her steel teeth, locked in perpetual metallic dialogue with a silver brooch like a figure-of-eight doggy doo that she wore at her collar, took the polished one-and-a-half-yard pointer in her hands and made purposefully for the dusty color-printed poster hanging to one side of the classroom. Holding the pointer like a rapier, she thrust its end into the unyielding word "International."

"Look over here, children," she said. "Children" was how she referred to her charges, demurring both from the school's "girls" and the faceless modernity of "kids." "We have here a picture of representatives of all the peoples of our great multinational motherland. Look, here are Russians and Ukrainians and Georgians and"—Lily sat back, half looking away in mute horror; was she really going to say it, making the whole class turn to stare at her?—"Tatars," the teacher continued. Everybody turned to stare instead at Raia Akhmetova, whose face flushed with dark blood. But Antonina Vladimirovna continued her headlong progress down the same dangerous path. "And Armenians and Azerbizhanis"—she actually said that, rather than "Azerbaijanis," she's not going to, she's not going to, ohmygod!—"and Jews!"

Lily froze. The entire class turned to stare at her.

Antonina Vladimirovna was a holy fool, a thoroughbred plebeian descended from a sacristan grandfather and a mother who took in washing. She was a spinster with a note on her medical file,

"*Virgina intacta,*" and had adopted an orphan—squint-eyed, ill-natured Zoika—during the war. She was an admirer of Chernyshevsky, with all his nineteenth-century didacticism, and worshiped, a feminist before her time, at the shrine of the women of social democracy, Klara Zetkin, Rosa Luxemburg, and Nadezhda Krupskaia. She believed in "the primacy of matter" as fervently as her grandfather the sacristan had believed in the Immaculate Conception, was as transparently honest as a pane of glass, and knew for a fact that while enemies no doubt were enemies, Jews were nevertheless simply Jews.

Lily failed to register the magnanimity of her gesture, conscious only of being stuck to the gloss-painted school bench by the strip of bare leg between her too short stockings and the tight elastic of her hated blue panties of itchy Chinese flannel.

"And all our peoples are equal." Antonina Vladimirovna continued her sacred pedagogic duty. "There is no such thing as a bad people. Every people has its heroes and its criminals, and even enemies of the people."

She rambled on and got off the point, but Lily was no longer listening. She could feel a little vein throbbing beside her nose and touched the place, trying to decide whether Svetka Bagaturiia, who sat across the aisle from her, would be able to see it pulsing.

***

As she neared the school gate, Lily discovered she was in luck: Bodrik wasn't there. She went skipping home with a sense of complete liberation, never stopping to think that he might be back tomorrow. The door to their flats, usually held tightly closed by a strong spring, was today slightly ajar, but Lily dismissed the fact. She threw it open and, stepping from light into darkness, was able to make out only the dark silhouette of a man standing by the inner door. It was Bodrik. He had been holding the door slightly open with his foot so as to see her as she came in.

There were two yards of pitch darkness separating them, but

she could see that for some reason he was standing with his back pressed against the inner door, his arms spread out in a cross, and his head with its thick hair inclined to one side.

He was an actor, Bodrik, and now he was playing a great and terrible role, which he thought was Christ, when in fact it was that of a sad, brazen little thug. Opposite him stood a girl with a dolorous Semitic face, a delicate, high-bridged nose, eyes that slanted down at the corners, a caring, full-lipped mouth, the incarnation of Joseph's Mary.

"What did you Jews want to go crucifying our Christ for, then?" he asked sarcastically. From his tone you would have thought that Jesus had been crucified by the Jews specifically so that he, Bodrik, should have a God-given right to wallop Lily's backside with a rusty iron gate.

She froze in anticipation, as if forgetting that she could yet run back out into the courtyard and take to her heels. The main entrance door was just behind her, but for some reason she stood transfixed.

Bodrik lunged forward, put his arms tightly round her, and slid his hands down. He pulled up her coat, which was unbuttoned, and pawed that same strip of bare leg between her stocking and where the elastic of her panties was pulled up right into her groin.

She wriggled free, rushed over to one corner, and rammed her briefcase into a soft part of Bodrik. He gasped. In the total darkness she unerringly found the door handle and ran outside. A vivid pink flame flared in her head, the air burst into flames around her, and such crimson rage suffused everything about that she shook violently, barely able to contain the immensity of an emotion that she could not name but which knew no bounds.

The door slowly opened and, shoulder first, slightly off balance, Bodrik emerged. She hurled herself at him, seized him by the shoulders, and with a shriek smashed him back against the door as hard as she could. The surprise of the attack completely bewildered him. The feelings he had long felt toward her, a mixture of attraction, spite, and an unacknowledged envy of her clean, well-fed life, were no match for the strength and inner conviction of the unadulterated rage seething in her soul.

He tried to break away and shake her off, but couldn't. He couldn't even take a proper swing to land a punch on her. He only succeeded in maneuvering himself round the corner from the entrance door into an alcove in the wall where at least they were not in full view of people walking through the courtyard. Even this was not to his advantage. She shook him by the shoulders and now beat his head against rough gray stone. His teeth began chattering, and he succeeded only in freeing one hand and drawing it twice down her sweating red face, not even like a man with the fist clenched, but open, leaving four shameful dirty scratch marks. She did not even feel it. She kept hurling him back against the wall, until suddenly the rage broke free from her like an inflated red balloon and drifted away. Then she let him go, turned an undefended back, and without crediting him with the initiative to attack her from behind, returned to the entrance to the flats without further hindrance.

***

How she had fancied him last summer. She had stood behind Grandmother's net curtains watching him for hours as he waved his long pole with the cloth flapping on the end of it, his doves rising lazily, circling above the dove cote like a disorderly crowd before forming up, making great, smooth circles that grew wider and wider, and then flying away into the clean, washed summer sky. She would slow down deliberately as she walked past the place where the Bodrovs lived, a shack with only two windows and with the dove cote, a shed for the rabbits, and a chicken coop tacked onto it. She would eye the fascinating intimate details of somebody else's private life: the iron kegs, the workbench at which the elder Bodrov busied himself, having recently emerged to a no doubt short-lived spell of freedom from his more traditional state of incarceration, the rusty water heater left lying outside.

At the end of the summer Bela Zinovievna, who relentlessly observed anachronistic obligations of the rich toward the poor that only she remembered about, sent Lily to the yard keeper's house with a starchily ironed and neatly folded pile of the clothes that Lily kept precipitously outgrowing that year. The Bodrov girls, Nina and Niusha, divided up Lily's goodies with much shrieking and whooping. Tonia the yard keeper thanked Lily and pressed a small green cucumber into her hand, but Bodrik, who had seen her coming in the distance, took himself off to his doves and rabbits and chickens. The whole time she was in their little territory fenced off from the rest of the courtyard he never showed himself. Lily kept looking over to see whether perhaps he was going to come out.

Only now, as she stood in the entrance to their smart flats, did she realize that that had been the most humiliating thing for him.

***

Old Nastia, who had lived with them some twenty years, was not home. Lily had been going to climb into bed with her great-grandfather, but he was sound asleep, snoring occasionally, and manifestly indifferent to her plight. She ran through to Grandmother's room, to the "divan of woe" as Bela Zinovievna called the chaise longue, the only item not duplicated in her realm of doubles, where everything came in twos, as if the room were divided by an invisible mirror. There were two proud beds ornamented with bronze, two bedside tables, and two marginally different pictures in identical frames. On this divan of woe Lily would sleep if she was ill, when Grandmother would take her into her own room, and she would come to cry on it when something happened in her young life to upset her.

Now she was feverish. She had an ache somewhere below her stomach, and she rolled up on the divan, drawing over her head the heavy check dressing gown with its twined and fraying purple cord. She just wanted to sleep, and sleep she did, instantly, still remembering, even in sleep, how much she wanted to sleep.

She slept for a long time, but through it all there ran a nagging sense of pain and utter revulsion. Revulsion at the coarseness of the divan's pillow, revulsion at the soapy smell of Red Moscow, Grandmother's favorite perfume, with its indecent suggestion of underwear. Overlaying it all was a boundless longing to escape into a warm, round hiding place she had always known was there, where she could sink into a deeper sleep and where there would be neither perfume nor pain nor this unsettling sense of shame that she could not understand, a place where there would be nothing, just nothing.

She did not hear the muffled activity around her grandfather through the wall, Nastia's sobs, the quiet clatter of a hypodermic needle. Great-grandfather Aaron was in a bad way.

Very late, at eight o'clock in the evening, she was wakened by her grandmother, and she must have succeeded in escaping far, far away, because when she awoke she could not at once tell where she was, so distant was the place from which she had to return to the paired symmetry and orderly world of Grandmother's room. She was startled by the bright face above her, which seemed unrecognizable and back to front, as if the recesses of sleep where she had dwelt were so singular as to exclude any possibility of pairing or symmetry.

Bela Zinovievna, for her part, was examining with undisguised amazement four fresh scratch marks that ran right from Lily's forehead, across her cheeks, and down to her chin.

"Good Lord, Lily. What has happened to your face?" she asked.

Lily had to think for a moment, so completely had she forgotten the events of the day. Then, all at once, everything came back to her, what had happened today, and the week before, and last summer, but it was wholly altered, unrecognizable and—completely unimportant. It was all just silly nonsense that had taken place a long time ago and that was already half forgotten.

"Oh, it's nothing. I had a bit of a fight with Bodrik," Lily answered nonchalantly, a smile on her sleepy face.

"What do you mean, a bit of a fight?" Bela Zinovievna demanded.

"Some drivel about why we crucified Christ," Lily said with a smile.

"What?" Bela Zinovievna exclaimed, knitting her black brows, and without waiting for a reply she told Lily to get dressed straightaway.

An afterglow of the anger that had swept over Lily by the entrance door now suffused her grandmother.

"How low. What rank ingratitude!" Bela Zinovievna raged, dragging the reluctant Lily to the Bodrovs' shack. It wasn't just the neat thirty-ruble notes that Bela Zinovievna punctually gave each holiday to this unfortunate drink-sodden mother who had fallen so low, nor the piles of her Lily's still perfectly presentable hand-me-downs. What offended against her symmetrical ideas of fairness was the very idea of Tonia's son raising his hand against her pure, unclouded little girl, profaning her with his dirty touch, inflicting these horrible scratches on her little dusky pink face. (She would have to remember to bathe them with permanganate.)

Bela Zinovievna knocked and flung the rickety door open without more ado. It was impossible to tell immediately what and who was where in the room, with its large stove and lines laden with damp washing. The stench of the poverty was dreadful, a blend of urine, mold, fungus, and seaweed. Worse even than Red Moscow.

"Tonia!" Bela Zinovievna called imperiously, and something rustled behind the stove.

Lily looked round to either side. What most struck her was the floor. It was earthen, with an intermittent covering of uneven boards. In a corner, on a broad iron bed with rusty bars exactly like those of the school railings, Bodrik was lying on a colored blanket. At his feet sat Nina and Niusha, winding broad crumpled ribbons onto the bedstead, painstakingly spitting on them before each wind. On the floor beside the bed stood a dented basin that had once been round.

Stocky little Tonia emerged rather unsteadily from behind the stove, straightening her skirt as she came.

"Here I am, Belzinovna!" she smiled, and on each cheek of her broad, flat face there appeared large dimples, as round as a belly button.

"Just look what your Victor has done to my little girl!" Bela Zinovievna said severely, while Tonia strained her whitish eyes and still could not make out what that was. In the dim light the scratches that had so incensed Bela Zinovievna really were barely visible. Lily retreated toward the door, abashed. Bodrik rolled his head, leaned over from the bed, and quietly puked into the basin.

"Oh, you shit!" Tonia shouted, turning on her son. "Get up, will you? What are you sprawling about there for!"

Neither of them spoke as they crossed the courtyard. Lily again trailed behind and again felt as bad as she had earlier before falling asleep. When she got back home, she went to the toilet, locked the door, and sat on the lavatory clutching her aching belly. Never before had she felt so ill. She looked down at her pants and saw a tulip-shaped bloodstain on their sky-blue material.

"I am dying," she guessed. "What a dreadful, shameful way to go."

At that moment she forgot everything her grandmother had warned her would happen. She pulled her soiled pants off in disgust and shoved them under the upturned bucket for washing the floors. She hid her scratched face in her cold hands and waited for death as her heart turned to glass.

***

Goaded by her expectation, Death came to the house at last. On his carpet-covered divan, old Aaron the shoemaker was drawing his last infrequent breaths. He was unconscious. His eyelids, which had long since lost their eyelashes, were not completely shut, but his eyes were not visible, only a cloudy, whitish film.

His withered hands lay above the quilt, and the worn-out leather straps were still wound round his left hand from which, against his custom, he had not removed them for a month. His children, the professors, burdened with much useless medical knowledge, stood by his bedside.

In the yard sweeper's house, on his iron bed, lay Bodrik, suffering from mild concussion.

On his narrow couch in a house in the countryside near Moscow, half covered by an old army blanket, another man lay dead.

But it was still only March 2, and several vast days would pass before Lily's father, the son of decent parents, would step out onto wooden boards, his face puffy, his heart black with grief, his epaulettes an innocent light blue, to announce to a gray rectangle of many thousands of men, one part of a great people that had been lost in a distant place, not registered by the botched color printing on the garish poster on the wall of Lily's classroom, that Comrade Stalin was dead.

That night, however, everybody forgot about a little girl who had locked herself in the toilet.

TRANSLATED FROM THE RUSSIAN

BY ARCH TAIT

Holy Fire

Carl Friedman

Carl Friedman was born in 1952 in Eindhoven, Netherlands, and is the daughter of a Holocaust survivor. After spending many years living in Belgium, she now resides in Amsterdam, where she works as a poet, translator, and novelist. Her first book, Tralievader *(Nightfather), was published in 1991 and became an international best seller. Her collection of stories* De grauwe minnaar *(1996) is available in English under the title* The Gray Lover *(1998).*

Her 1993 novel Twee koffers vol *(The Shovel and the Loom) was made into the film* Left Luggage, *which won, among other prizes, the Blue Angel Award. The principal character of the novel is the young philosophy student Chaya, who lives in the Jewish quarter of Antwerp, Belgium. Like many of Friedman's female protagonists, Chaya is intimately familiar with the history of Jewish thought and literature. She studies Issac Luria, a sixteenth-century cabalist from Safed, in northern Israel, and gains a new understanding of life in the Diaspora: "With the dispersion of the divine light began the Diaspora of the Jews, whose task it was to gather the stray sparks and in that way restore the cosmos to its former perfection. According to Luria, this restoration could be expedited by study of the Torah and obedience to divine commands. . . . Under the influence of Luria, the Diaspora became a positive force, the condition for, as well as the introduction to,* Olam Haba, *the World to Come. The person of the Messiah became less important. The crucial thing was to prepare his way."*

✳

This is the story of Hans Levie and the transformation that he underwent. Although it was not as spectacular as the metamorphosis of Gregor Samsa, who, according to Kafka, awoke one morning as a monstrous cockroach, to this day Hans's parents have not recovered from their fright, and maybe they never will.

Through my long friendship with his mother, Miriam, I have watched Hans grow up, from his first steps to his first bicycle, from nursery school to high school. I also spent several summer vacations with the Levies in Brittany, but what I remember most about those is the view of the windy beach and the sea, with Hans in the distant background, hanging on to a kite or up to his waist in a sandy hole. When he was sixteen, just before his life took a disastrous turn, Hans was an average boy with blond hair and rosy cheeks, dividing his attention between soccer and girls. He wasn't very clever. The postcards and the few letters from him that I have saved bristle with errors. Was I fond of him? I know only that I didn't find him particularly objectionable. I was rather indifferent to him. In retrospect I think that's unfortunate. If I'd paid more attention to him at the time, maybe now I'd be able to give an explanation, any explanation whatsoever, for his later behavior. But he wasn't the kind of boy who inspires curiosity. And anyway, perhaps it's an illusion that we, who understand so little about ourselves, can truly fathom what possesses others.

I met Miriam in 1971. One evening in February she showed up at my door, very pregnant and rain drenched. She had, she explained, searched the local telephone directory page by page for Jewish last names, and now she was dropping in on those people, hoping to interest them in getting together.

"Getting together?" I asked suspiciously. "To do what?"

"To exchange ideas with kindred spirits. With people to whom you don't have to explain anything and from whom you don't have to hide anything. And to whom you can tell your best

Jewish joke with confidence." She made this speech as though she'd practiced it at home.

"My best Jewish joke? I'm no good at telling jokes."

"How do you like this one?" she said. "Jake says to Sam that he wants to be baptized. 'What a disgrace,' says Sam, 'your father will turn over in his grave.' Says Jake, 'That's all right, my brother is getting baptized next week, and then Father will be on his back again.'"

I waved my hand; I knew a much better one.

Laughing, we walked to the kitchen, and before long we were engaged in a passionate discussion about ginger shortbread, herring salad, and books by Bernard Malamud.

The first meeting was held in Miriam and her husband Alex's house. They had just moved in. Amidst the chaos of the enclosed porch, where cardboard boxes were stacked everywhere, those present shyly sat together while a parrot screeched: "Hello, raisin bun; hello, raisin bun." We were six, including the host and hostess. The idea was for all of us to introduce ourselves and then briefly say something about our past.

There was Thérèse Twersky, in her early fifties, originally French, a potter, elegant and lively. She said that she didn't actually know why she had accepted Miriam's invitation. She was only moderately interested in Judaism. But she was fascinated by Buddhism and by other exotic religions. She had just returned from a trip to Mexico, where, searching for inspiration, she had studied classic Native American ceramics. When she spoke at too great length about the differences between Olmec, Zapotec, Chichimik, and Aztec pottery, Miriam firmly took over.

Then there were Isidore Galatzer and his wife, Rose, both short, stocky, originally from Romania. They were the same age as Thérèse. Rose was in a wheelchair. A result of the war, she explained. She'd been imprisoned in Vertujeni, a Romanian concentration camp where the only food was a cattle feed that caused gradual paralysis. Upon liberation she'd had to leave the camp by crawling on her knees. She'd lost all strength in her leg muscles. In addition she could barely move her left arm.

"Compared to Vertujeni," she said, "Auschwitz was a vacation spot."

"Oh, really," said Thérèse indignantly. "If I'd only known sooner. I would have taken along my bathing suit and suntan cream."

"Were you in Auschwitz?" Miriam asked.

Thérèse nodded.

"At least you got some bread," said Isidore to Thérèse. "We got absolutely nothing. The Romanians didn't need the Germans to get rid of the Jews. They did it themselves; they did it on Romanian soil and as cheaply as possible. Trains, gas chambers, bread rations—they thought that was money down the drain. Jews weren't even worth kicking to death. We had to be destroyed, but without costing a cent. They made us walk enormous distances. Whoever didn't collapse from exhaustion on the way would starve later in the camp. I was imprisoned in Dumanovka. There, we ate grass. But I escaped. For a year I hid in the forests. Underground, like a rat in a hole. I almost went crazy."

"Isidore hates anything that's Romanian," said Rose. "He doesn't even allow me to sing Romanian songs."

"The only good Romanian is a dead Romanian," shouted Isidore, his face red with excitement. "There wasn't one Romanian who helped me, not one."

Thérèse kept silent, and I stared into my coffee cup.

Miriam, who saw her carefully prepared evening beginning to fall apart, gathered all her courage. "I was *most certainly* helped," she said with emphasis. "By a miner's family in Limburg. With nine children. I was hidden there until the end of the war. They lived in a small, dilapidated house, and they all slept in the attic. I was four years old and had lived in an enormous mansion in The Hague. So when I stepped over the threshold in Limburg, the first thing I exclaimed was, 'Where is the sofa? Where is the piano?'"

We laughed, all except Isidore. Sighing, he loosened his tie and undid the collar of his shirt.

"They were sweet people," said Miriam. "They had no fear. In the village, I went to school normally, supposedly as their niece from a northern province. For my own protection they taught me to say the Hail Mary. I still know it."

Speaking more to herself than us, she began in a singsong voice: "Hail Mary, full of grace, the Lord be with you. . . ."

"Hello, raisin bun," the parrot shouted irreverently.

"I get enticed to come here under the pretense of a Jewish gathering," muttered Isidore, "and then they recite the Hail Mary."

Relieved, everyone started talking at once. Alex threw me an understanding look across the table. We were the only ones who hadn't said a word yet.

I soon became attached to our little group assembled by chance from the telephone book. Alex and Miriam, Isidore and Rose, Thérèse and I were the faithful ones from the very beginning. In those early days an alliance was established among us that remained indestructible through the years, even after our numbers increased and we got membership administration and bookkeeping, our own house of prayer, a cantor, and a part-time rabbi.

Alex took on the task of secretary. Miriam and Thérèse started to learn Hebrew and soon became quite proficient. Isidore became treasurer, while Rose, using only one hand, embroidered a beautiful mantle for the brand-new Torah scroll. But I kept apart. I rarely showed up in the synagogue. The services lasted too long, and even though I tried to let myself be carried away by the prayers, they never became more than protocol for me. Once in a while, on holidays, I would go anyway, but chiefly to nestle next to Thérèse and to enjoy the intimacy of our leafing together through one prayer book. Or to experience one of the few occasions when Isidore pressed against his wife's wheelchair and spread his prayer shawl over her head and his own. At that moment they seemed like normal people who had never heard of Vertujeni or Dumanovka. Under the white silk tallith they looked as delighted as children who, under the covers, tell each other their deepest secrets and who peek out from between the sheets only to make sure that no one is eavesdropping.

None of them blamed me for not attending the services and the meetings regularly.

"You aren't suited for organization life," Miriam said with a certain tenderness. "That's hardly a crime, is it?"

Isidore was even proud of what he called my independence. "If you ever have to sit in a pit in the woods, you'll stay completely sane." He nodded contentedly. "You don't need anyone; you'll manage quite well."

The truth was that I wouldn't have known what to do without them. I have never felt at home anywhere the way I did with them. I'm not easy on myself and certainly not on others. They knew how to love me and, what's more, to do so effortlessly.

A few weeks after Hans's sixteenth birthday, Miriam called me. She asked me whether I was interested in a lecture about Solomon Ibn Gabirol. She explained that Gabirol was a Jewish scholar from the Spanish Middle Ages and that he had written poems that had become part of the service.

"Next week, Sunday," she said, "in Amsterdam. It starts at two o'clock in the afternoon, so we have to leave here at noon."

Then she lowered her voice.

"Do you know that Hans is no longer going to school? He's already been at home for four days. I have to speak softly because he's walking around here somewhere."

"Cutting school happens in the best families," I said.

"No, it's not cutting school. He's refusing to stay in that school. He says that it's a stupid, provincial school for farmhands. He complains that we've moved to Groningen, where he now has to waste his life. 'How could you have done that to me?' he says. As if we are in the middle of the Sahara or the jungle."

"Is he having problems with a teacher or something?"

"I thought so at first, but I called the school, and there's nothing wrong. No, it's much deeper. He feels that this isn't a city for Jews. There's no Yiddishkeit here, he says."

"Hans and Yiddishkeit?" I laughed. "Since when does he

worry about Yiddishkeit? He doesn't even know the difference between Abraham and Moses."

"I don't understand it either. In the beginning I thought, Don't worry, it's adolescence; others suffer from acne and your son suffers from Yiddishkeit. But he's dead serious. He's suddenly brought home all sorts of books about Judaism."

"Brought home? Don't you already have enough books about it?"

"No, he doesn't think much of our books. They're too liberal for him."

"It's hard to believe. Especially since he always disliked religion so much."

"Yes, I know. He never wanted anything to do with it. He wanted to be like the other children in his class. How often did he pester me about a Christmas tree and Easter eggs? On Saturdays, when we went to Sabbath service, he went to the soccer field. We always let him do whatever he liked. And now this."

"What does Alex think of it?"

"You know Alex. He has no patience at all for these things. In the evening he comes home from work dead tired and pushes everything off on me. Yesterday he said, 'You give in too easily. Be firm and send that boy back to school.'"

There was silence for a moment. She heaved a big sigh.

"I don't know," she said. "Maybe he's right. I did become a mother very late in life."

"Nonsense," I said. "That's typically female. A man looks at us with reproach, and we go and stand in the corner of our own free will. Women have an overdeveloped sense of guilt. Why doesn't *Alex* stand firm? Why doesn't *Alex* send Hans back to school? Isn't Hans his son too?"

"Yes, but Hans won't have anything to do with his old school. He just wants to go to a Jewish school."

"Then he's out of luck. There are no Jewish schools in this city."

"He's made calls to schools in Antwerp and Amsterdam."

"But how can he go there? He has his final examinations next year. For sixteen years he didn't care about Yiddishkeit, so it can't be terribly urgent. Maybe it will pass. Let him finish the school year."

The tone of Miriam's voice changed. "That's settled then," she said cheerfully. "You're going with us to Amsterdam. Thérèse is also coming. Rose is still considering; she's always afraid to be a bother to others with her wheelchair."

"Is Hans around?" I asked, whispering in spite of myself.

"Yes," she exclaimed, "I'll take care of transportation. Alex can easily do without the car for an evening."

"Good," I said, "we'll discuss this another time. We should definitely talk about it again."

But she had already hung up with a quick good-bye.

In the afternoon I bicycled to Thérèse's studio. Although almost seventy, she still worked every day. She was at the potter's wheel in the back of the room, her gray hair down her back in a careless braid. I liked to watch while under her hands pots and pitchers made their shining pirouettes.

"*Ma petite,*" she said without looking up.

"Am I interrupting?"

"*Pas du tout.*" She stopped the wheel. "It's not working today."

She went to wash up at the sink and took off her apron.

"It's always something nowadays," she said. "If it isn't my shoulders, then it's my back. Souvenirs of Auschwitz."

With disdain, she looked at the bowl she had made.

"See, I create new things. But I myself am cracked."

Still, she seemed amazingly intact for someone her age. She possessed the tough flexibility of a ballerina. In the most shapeless sweater she appeared distinguished.

Together we stood in front of the window. She pointed to the crown of a tall maple in which the outline of a dome-shaped nest was visible.

"That belongs to two magpies," she said. "They build their nest with a roof, just like us, and they coat it with mud. A few months ago, when there was such a terrible storm, the whole nest fell down. The next morning they began all over again, twig by twig."

She put her arm around me.

"When it becomes too much for me," she said, "I look at that nest. Then I tell myself that I should be like the magpies. That I should live from day to day and do my work. Not look into the abyss, but continue. Just continue until the next storm."

We drank some coffee.

I asked her if she had heard that Hans was troubled by attacks of Yiddishkeit.

She knew about it but thought the matter hardly worth discussing. "A symptom of adolescence," she said with a nonchalant wave of her hand. "He's sixteen and wants to drive his parents up the wall."

"Well, then, he's succeeded," I said. "When Miriam called me this morning, she sounded very unhappy. She thinks she's failed as a mother."

Thérèse yawned.

"That's part of it," she said. "Did Miriam say anything to you about the lecture?"

I nodded.

"I promised that I'd come along," I said, "but I don't really feel like it."

"You don't feel like it?" she exclaimed. "It's a great opportunity. The lecturer is Benjamin Lemberg. A fantastic man and an authority. There is no one who knows as much about the Jewish poets of Spain as Lemberg. He's devoted his whole life to the subject."

"Yes, but he's coming to talk only about Gabirol. I'd rather hear something about the others. About Ha-Nagid, for example."

Thérèse, who didn't consider me qualified to express opinions about these matters, shrugged her shoulders patronizingly.

"Why Ha-Nagid?"

"Because he was practically everything at once. Philosopher and linguist, rabbi and poet. As vizier to the caliph of Granada, he became commander of the royal forces. A Jew at the head of an Islamic army—that speaks to my imagination. Twenty long years he fought. He won one battle after the other. You wonder how with all that din of clashing arms he found time for writing. Still, he wrote the most beautiful poetry."

Enthusiastically, I recited:

"Be brave in times of danger or sorrow,
even when standing at death's door.
A lamp glows brightest before the morrow.
Lions when wounded loudest roar."

"That certainly is beautiful," Thérèse admitted. "Where did you get that translation?"

My face flushed. "It's mine."

"Since when do you know Hebrew?"

"I learned it as a child."

"Why didn't you tell us?"

"I don't know. Maybe because I was afraid you'd expect all sorts of things from me."

"So while we took you for an illiterate, you sat at home secretly translating Ha-Nagid?"

"Promise not to tell the others," I said.

"Do you also read the Torah?"

"That too," I said reluctantly. "But don't misunderstand. I do it only because I like the sound of the language and the metaphors."

"You don't need to make excuses," said Thérèse. "Reading the Torah is not a punishable offense. The age of the Inquisition is past."

"I'm not making excuses at all. Why should I?"

"You yourself know that best, *ma petite.* Someone who translates Ha-Nagid isn't exactly stupid."

In fact, I did possess an excellent knowledge of the Torah and related matters, which I had concealed from the others in our group. My intention was to avoid the long prayer services and the joint study of scripture, but mostly I didn't want to be reminded of my past.

I grew up in an Orthodox family in Antwerp. My father, a pious Jew who earned his living by teaching Hebrew and the Talmud, dreamed of progeny consisting of nothing but rabbis and cantors. He would have preferred to raise twelve sons, like Jacob. When my mother, after several miscarriages, presented him with only one daughter, he could hardly swallow his disappointment. All his paternal ambition was concentrated on me. Evening after evening I sat bent over books from which he instructed me in the reading and explication of holy scripture.

Outside the house I was timid and awkward. I understood practically nothing about the world and its ways. Whatever I knew, I had taught myself and learned in secret. From the school library I took home novels in which there was not a word about God. In modern magazines I read articles about love, sexuality, and other matters that were barely mentioned in the Torah. Girlfriends in my classes listened to records by the Beatles and the Rolling Stones, uninhibited boys in tight pants who called things by their true names. Whereas in Genesis it says covertly, "And he came to her," they sang openly: "Treat me like you did the night before," and "I can't get no satisfaction."

For my father, worldly matters didn't seem to exist. His whole life, including the smallest everyday thing, was directed toward God. Judaism has prayers for almost everything—for bread and other food, for smells, colors, and sounds. My father used them all. He did that "because all that we enjoy here on earth is a gift from the Almighty, and therefore every pleasure, no matter how small, loses its value for us if we do not honor our Creator for it." He praised God for the taste of fresh coffee and for the chirping of innocent sparrows on the windowsill. He even said a blessing over the inkpot from which he filled his pen. Until deep into the night he sat bent over *The Guide for the Perplexed, The Source of Life,* and other mystical texts.

He took almost every word from the holy books literally. In this he went so far that he considered the earth as the center of the universe. Although even imbeciles had been convinced of the contrary for centuries, he maintained that the sun turned around the earth. He had established a society that, in addition to himself, had three members: a partially deaf neighbor, our kosher baker, and a retired fur dealer, all of whom frequented the same house of prayer as my father and upon whom he had imposed his eccentric point of view. They called themselves the Brothers of Gibeon, after the place where, according to scripture, the sun had stopped in the sky for a whole day at the command of Joshua. The meetings that the society held in our living room were noisy. My father always gave a long speech. He did that standing up while taking small, tripping steps like a boxer in the ring. His body swayed as though he were praying, and under the coat of his black suit, the white fringes of his prayer shirt began to tremble. His movements seemed threatening, like those of a boxer in the ring. Everything on him was in turmoil—even his glasses kept sliding to the tip of his nose. He quoted patriarchs, prophets, and cabalists, anyone who had written anything that suited his beliefs about the heavenly bodies. He let his voice surge to unprecedented volume, perhaps because he feared that his listeners, all being gentlemen of a certain age, would doze off.

My mother had reconciled herself to the existence of this crazy club, but my own opposition to it grew as I became older.

"You don't really think that the sun revolves around the earth?" I said to my father.

"I don't think so," he answered. "I know it for sure."

"And Kepler? And Galileo?"

"They were totally off the mark."

"You sound so certain—as if they were carpenters or ironmongers."

"That's probably true."

"And Newton?"

"What do you mean, Newton?" my father exclaimed vehemently. "I'm referring to texts that are thousands of years old. That Newton of yours is only a toddler compared to them, an insignificant nincompoop."

The gulf between my father and me constantly grew wider. On my eighteenth birthday, when I told him I wanted to become a journalist, the bomb exploded. He had hoped that I would marry, preferably Benjamin Kirschner, one of his students who clutched a prayer book to his chest wherever he went and who blushed when he met me. But my father realized that no God-fearing man would want to stand under the marriage canopy with a future journalist and, conversely, that no journalist would want to share her life with someone whose idea of the latest news was medieval Bible commentaries. After a terrible fight, I left the house for good. Alone, on a rented delivery bicycle loaded with bags and boxes, I disappeared from the sight of my weeping mother. At that moment the chances of my father's having a rabbi as a son-in-law evaporated. He never forgave me.

At my departure he cursed me from the bottom of his heart. He shouted at me, telling me that I was an ungrateful bitch and that outside the safety of the family I would amount to nothing. But he was as mistaken in this as he was in the movements of the heavenly bodies. I found a job at the *Northern Daily* in Groningen, where, after an internship, I got a permanent job on the national and foreign affairs editorial staff.

At first I kept in touch with my mother, but our infrequent correspondence soon came to an end. My father had sprinkled ashes on his head and said kaddish, the traditional prayer for the dead, for me. I no longer existed for him; I had become a spirit. He wouldn't allow my mother to keep in touch with me, and he referred to Leviticus, in which the God of Israel says, "And if any person turns to ghosts and familiar spirits and goes astray after them, I will set my face against that person and cut him off from among his people." That scared my mother thoroughly.

The last sign of life that I received from her was a parcel. It contained an old book, without a spine and spattered with grease. On the cover it said in worn gold letters *Ritual Cookbook.* When I opened it, a note in her neat, sloping handwriting fell out. She wrote that she had waited for years to give me this book, which had belonged to my grandmother. Now, to her unspeakable sadness, she was obliged to send it to me as a good-bye. She wished me luck with it and referred to page 151 for my favorite dish, kugel with pears.

The pages were tattered. The book had been published in 1932 under the supervision of two rabbis, a urologist, and a specialist in stomach, intestinal, and metabolic diseases. It contained references to Creation and to the Flood. Users of this book could not fry an egg without being reminded of the dangers of idolatry, murder, and lawlessness. The writers, the ladies Glück and Bramson, urged over and over again the strict observance of dietary laws and warned of spiritual degeneration. Was that the reason my mother had sent me this book? Did she hope to protect me from degeneration? As though the events after 1932 hadn't shown that there exists a degeneration that won't be restrained by anything or anyone, not by religious leaders or politicians and certainly not by a cookbook. The thought was almost touching in its innocence. I imagined the newspaper headlines: "The Ladies Glück and Bramson Cause the Fall of the Third Reich." "Jewish Cookbook Compulsory Reading for Germans." "Adolf Hitler Defeated by Kugel with Pears."

This was how matters stood. My father had declared me dead, and my mother, albeit reluctantly, had followed him in this. They had banished their daughter to the realm of the spirits. And as the years passed, they in turn became increasingly like spirits for me. What should I tell Alex, Miriam, and the others about my parents? We had cut ourselves off from each other.

During our outing in Amsterdam, Miriam was deliberately cheerful. She didn't mention Hans. And either because we didn't want to spoil the mood or because of cowardice, we avoided asking about him.

But in the months that followed, his name came up often, usually when anything changed in Miriam and Alex's household. Like the time we noticed they had gotten a new tea set.

"Lovely," I said.

"Pretty, those yellow flowers," said Rose, holding her cup up to the light.

But Thérèse, who had personally created the old tea service, asked, "What's wrong with the other one? Are you tired of it?"

"Well," said Miriam, avoiding Thérèse's eyes, "I wanted something different."

But later, when the subject of the discussion had changed, Miriam suddenly exclaimed, "It was washed away."

We didn't understand what she was talking about.

"Thérèse's tea set," explained Miriam. "I'd rather tell the truth. It was washed away."

"That doesn't surprise me at all," said Rose. "That dishwasher of yours has been making such strange noises."

"No," said Miriam, pointing toward the garden doors, "it washed away in the canal in back. It's because of Hans. He said that my dishes were not kosher and that I had to clean them."

"Clean them?" I asked, disbelieving. "In that canal? That's where the dirtiest factories discharge their waste products."

Miriam looked helpless. "He said that I had to immerse them in naturally running water. And the canal is the only naturally running water in the area. So I went there carrying bags filled with dishes, near the lock where the current is strongest."

"You must be crazy," said Thérèse.

"I did it because otherwise he wouldn't eat at home anymore. And we see so little of him as it is."

Meanwhile Hans was living in Antwerp, where he was completing high school in a strict religious school. He was boarding with a Hasidic family. Because his religious conviction made it impossible for him to travel on the Sabbath and because he had lessons on Sunday as well, he spent only his vacations at home.

"Was anything else washed away?" asked Thérèse.

"Not the pans," answered Miriam, "because they have handles. But almost everything else, including the knives and forks. Alex was angry with Hans, but Hans said that it was our own fault. 'Can I help it,' he said, 'that you live like unbelievers? You don't even know the simplest rules. If you lived in Antwerp, you wouldn't have these problems. Then the dishes wouldn't be lying at the bottom of the canal!'"

"And these new dishes?" worried Rose as she inspected the contents of her cup. "Did you clean them in the canal as well?"

"I don't dare anymore. We've found another solution. Hans brought pots with him that were cleaned in Antwerp under rabbinical supervision. He prepares his own meals in those, on an electric hot plate in his room. And he eats from plastic plates."

"*Mon Dieu!*" sighed Thérèse.

"Why do you give in to him in such idiotic things?" I wanted to know.

Feeling uneasy because of our vehement reactions, Miriam tightened her face. "I want to respect his views," she said stiffly. "Frederick the Great said everyone must find salvation in his own way. *Jeder soll selig werden nach seiner Façon.* And I completely agree with him."

"*Oh, la la,*" said Thérèse. "I didn't know that we'd be having tea with Frederick the Great."

"Is he kosher enough?" I teased. "Shouldn't you ask Hans's approval?"

"Which Frederick?" asked Rose, slow to understand as always.

We were all speaking at the same time.

Miriam shouted over everything: "You can say what you want, but I admire Hans. I admire his self-discipline. He used to be too damned lazy to sit and do his homework for even an hour. Now he can't get enough of it. All day long he's with his books, from early morning till late at night. It's hard work to be a good Jew, you can take that from me. He sacrifices everything for it."

"Even his own father and mother," snapped Thérèse.

"You don't understand," said Miriam. "It's as difficult for him as it is for us. He would rather just eat from my plates. But he can't do that; it goes against his principles."

"A sixteen-year-old who from one day to the next acquires holy principles and tyrannizes everyone around him with them?" said Thérèse. "*Je m'en fous.*"

"Hans has enormous dedication," Miriam said emphatically, perhaps to overcome her doubts. "A dedication that you seldom find nowadays. His ideas on Judaism don't necessarily match ours, but at any rate he lives according to them. Many people could follow his example."

At these last words she looked at me sideways.

Dejected, we were silent. Some minutes passed.

Rose, who had only half understood, tried to get the conversation going again.

"Nice dishes," she said awkwardly. "So sunny, with those yellow flowers."

Miriam rubbed her face wearily.

"You think so? Well, it's a change."

We had expected that Alex, being sarcastic and inflexible, would bring Hans in line. But that didn't happen. To our great amazement Alex became only more accommodating. Perhaps he didn't want to spoil the little time that Hans spent at home by having fights, which might alienate the boy even further. Perhaps he feared resistance from Miriam, who was plagued by feelings of guilt and ready to give in to the boy in everything. But he probably thought, as we did, that Hans's Yiddishkeit was nothing more than a way to rebel against his parents. After all, what did Isidore, Rose, Thérèse, and I know about children? Because we ourselves were childless, we withheld our judgment of those who had been bold enough to have them.

But we weren't blind. And although we joked about it among ourselves, it was not without concern that we noticed how rapidly the strict mores that Hans learned in Antwerp took over the parental home. At his urging, a mezuzah appeared on almost every doorpost. At his urging, the walls were purged of all images that were offensive to Orthodox notions, so that most paintings were banished to the attic. At his urging, Miriam started wearing clothes that covered her arms below the elbows and her legs below the knees. At his urging, Alex gave up drinking whiskey and got rid of his wine cellar. At every meeting we saw the compelling hand of Hans. Had the magazines on the coffee table been replaced by a massive reference work about Jewish ethics? Hans must be behind that. Did an enormous eight-branched candelabrum appear in the windowsill? Hans must have placed it there. Isidore, Rose, Thérèse, and I silently threw each other glances in which the same word could be read every time: *Hans, Hans, Hans.*

Finally even the parrot disappeared.

"Where did Yupi go?" asked Isidore, shocked, during one of our get-togethers.

He was standing in the enclosed porch in the place where the cage had been for years. The hand he had lifted to scratch the parrot's neck between the feathers dropped limply.

Alex squirmed with embarrassment.

"Hmm, Yupi," he said, surprised, as though he hadn't noticed the absence of the parrot before this.

Miriam came to his rescue.

"Yupi was annoying," she said. "Every time Hans started his afternoon prayer, Yupi would screech through it. You know what a racket he could make. Not a sensible word came out. All day long it was, 'Hello, raisin bun; hello, raisin bun.'"

She laughed, but Isidore stiffened.

"You're not going to tell me that you got rid of Yupi?"

"We didn't get rid of him," said Alex. "We found him a home with a real fancier, someone with five other parrots and a cockatoo."

"Wait a minute," said Isidore, "this is beyond me. Yupi has always made a racket, as long as I've been coming to your house. And suddenly, because the animal can't pray, he has to disappear?"

"Yupi was a difficult case," said Miriam. "We couldn't figure out whether he was an unclean bird, but Hans had his suspicions. The Talmud says nothing about parrots, but with that curved beak and those claws on their legs, they resemble birds of prey. And birds of prey are not allowed."

"Are not allowed by whom?" Isidore exclaimed angrily.

"By the rabbinate."

"Perhaps *eating* parrots is forbidden," said Isidore, "but you're still allowed to keep them as pets."

"That's permitted, but Hans says that it isn't wise to surround yourself with unclean animals."

Isidore's eyes filled with tears. "But didn't God create these animals himself? If Hans can do it better, why doesn't he organize his own creation, somewhere in a remote spot? A world for him alone, without parrots. And also without his father and mother, because they no longer seem to be able to do anything right in his eyes."

"What are you saying?" Alex shouted, agitated.

"Oh, please," hushed Miriam.

"No," Alex said bitterly. "No, he's going too far. He shouldn't interfere with our family life. This is my house, and I'm the boss here. What I do with my parrot or with my son is none of his damned business!"

Isidore gasped for breath.

"Don't get excited," whispered Rose. "Please, think of your heart."

Thérèse, to restore the peace, asked the quarreling parties to sit down and count to one hundred. But Isidore shook his head.

"I wish you had given Yupi to us," he said regretfully as he pushed the wheelchair with Rose in it away. "We thought he was a sweet bird. We would have liked to take him home. For that we don't have to consult the rabbinate, not us."

Without saying good-bye he left the house with his wife. It was the first time that our group had been divided by a quarrel.

Ever since Hans had gone to live in Antwerp we hadn't seen him at all. That could hardly be accidental. I suspected that Alex and Miriam had arranged it that way. Whenever Hans spent a vacation in Holland, they scrupulously kept Rose, Isidore, Thérèse, and me away from their house. Were they afraid that their son would be offended by our liberal behavior? Or did they worry that we would be chased away by his pious talk? They obviously thought nothing good could come from a confrontation, and they were probably right.

Even when he finished high school, we didn't get to see Hans. In the summer, after he had passed his final examinations, he left for New York. He had enrolled in an institute for Talmudic studies in Brooklyn. Miriam glowed with pride. On the Sabbath after his departure, she came up to us in the synagogue. The service was over. We stood around talking over a cup of coffee.

"Did you hear?" she asked triumphantly. "Hans is studying in America now."

We congratulated her warmly.

"He already has quite a few friends over there," she told us, "because he's joined Chabad."

"He joined what?" asked Rose.

"Chabad," repeated Miriam.

"A Hasidic sect," I said, "that goes into the streets in buses to bring disaffected Jews back to the faith."

"It's not a sect," said Miriam, offended. "It's a movement."

I shrugged my shoulders. "A sect or a movement, it all comes down to the same thing."

"They're two very different things," Miriam said, piqued.

"At any rate," I said, continuing my explanation to Rose, "an ancient rabbi is at the head of it. His name is Menachem Mendel Schneerson, and he has proclaimed himself prophet or Messiah, or both. He has visions and he makes predictions. Some say he's holy. Others, like me, think that he's a charlatan."

Miriam protested. "Schneerson has already cured thousands of the sick with his prayers!"

"Yes," I said, "he performs healing work for humanity, but he doesn't do it for nothing. He expects to be paid for each prayer."

"Why does that matter?" said Miriam. "Don't doctors ask money for a treatment?"

I nodded. "Of course. But a doctor has had training. Schneerson is unqualified."

"He doesn't need training," she said, "because he is a seer. His knowledge is innate. He seems to be a descendant of King David."

I burst out laughing. "That's a well-known trick. In Jewish history there have been droves of false prophets and messiahs. One passed himself off as Moses, another one claimed that he was Daniel or Elijah. They were braggarts and swindlers who had delusions of grandeur. Everywhere they spread stories about

their so-called superhuman powers until they themselves started
believing them. Most died a violent death, just like Christ, who
is also supposed to be descended directly from King David."

"That's possible," said Miriam, "but does it mean that Schneerson is a swindler? He has followers all over the world."

"A following is not proof of reliability. Every false messiah has
followers. Some have had millions. Joseph Stalin, Adolf Hitler,
Mao Tse-tung."

"Yes, if that's how you think!" she said, offended. She turned
away and joined another group.

Rose moved restlessly in her wheelchair.

"I don't understand it at all," she said. "Is that Sneepson a
rabbi or a doctor?"

Isidore repeated, partly in Romanian, partly in Yiddish, what
we had said.

"Well, it won't come to that," said Thérèse. "Hans is a Dutch
boy. He is much too sensible to let himself be carried away by a
clairvoyant messiah. I've lived in this country for twenty years,
and I've never yet seen anyone be carried away. *Ils sont trop fleg-
matiques, les Néerlandais.* They don't have strong feelings. That is
their weakness and their strength."

Isidore said in a muffled voice, "Good riddance. Let him stay
in New York, then he can't upset Alex and Miriam."

Rose looked worried. "And what if you're all wrong?" she
said. "What if that Sneepson turns out to be the Messiah?"

"We'll be able to tell without any problem," said Thérèse,
mockingly, "from the sound of the trumpets."

"And the wolf shall lie down with the lamb," I declared. "And
a child shall stretch out his hand over the eye of a viper."

"I'll drink to that," said Isidore as he tossed down his last sip
of coffee.

***

Not long after that, I received in my mail a letter that appeared
to come from Hans. In his almost illegible writing he urged me
to hasten the coming of the Messiah. I could do this, he wrote

in a childish and sloppy Dutch, by not smoking cigarettes, by not drinking, and by sanctifying the Sabbath. He reminded me that I belonged to a people with a task who must enlighten the world, a people who has produced thinkers like Spinoza, Freud, Einstein, and many others, mentioning one after the other by their full names, so that his letter resembled a page from the telephone book.

I felt offended, not so much by the message, but by the arrogance of the messenger. Who did this conceited adolescent think he was? My response was short but scathing. I opened with a quote from Franz Kafka: "The Messiah will come only when he is no longer needed, he will only come one day after his arrival, he will not come on the last day but on the very last."

Underneath it I wrote that the Jewish people had indeed produced impressive thinkers but that someone like Hans, who couldn't even spell their names correctly, was hardly justified in feeling related to them, let alone in boasting of such a relationship. "It's true," I wrote, "that the world can use some more light. But not all Jews carry a torch, just as not all torchbearers are Jewish." I was going to mention the names of Erasmus, Dante, and so on, down to Chekhov, but I changed my mind. From one of my desk drawers I dug up a few twenty-dollar bills, which I enclosed with my letter. "Do something nice with the money," I advised him in a postscript. "Have you seen the new Woody Allen film yet?"

Later, Miriam said that Hans had been hurt by my letter because I had quoted a *German* writer. Apparently he was unaware of the fact that Franz Kafka had lived in Prague and was one of the thinkers, according to him, on whom Jewish history possesses an exclusive patent. Miriam also told me that he had spent my dollars on gas to fill up the tank of the van he used to roam the streets of New York looking for converts. I had financed the missionary work of Schneerson.

Hans stayed in the United States during the whole winter and the following spring. He no longer sent me moralizing letters, but, as befits a good missionary, he didn't lose heart after only one attempt. He gave me ample opportunity to save my immortal soul. With a certain regularity I received English-language magazines and colorful flyers. I never let him know that they had reached me, but I did read them. They were curious propaganda leaflets. We were living, the writers claimed over and over again, in an age of sin and destruction. Creation was thoroughly corrupt. Everywhere in the world people were engaged in slandering, whoring, and cutting each other's throats to their hearts' content, although the Almighty had expressly forbidden this. Fortunately the great change was in sight. The end of time was nearing, Mashiach was preparing to establish the kingdom of David on earth and to rebuild the destroyed Temple. A horrible fate awaited sinners who did not repent in time. Women would be afflicted by scabies, men would be felled by the sword, and if that weren't sufficient, then they all would be consumed by flames.

The illustrations looked familiar to me. Not only were they hardly distinguishable from the pictures in the magazine of the Jehovah's Witnesses, but they also looked suspiciously like the illustrations on book covers and posters of Hitler's time. Stiffly drawn men and women, impeccably dressed and with their hair still wet from their baths, resolutely turned their eyes to the heavens. *We have placed our hope in the Lord. Führer, wir folgen.*

Sometime in June, Miriam called me. She was exuberant, like a young girl.

"Hans is coming home next week," she said happily, "and to share his knowledge with others, he wants to invite all of you. Are you free on Thursday evening?"

I had no desire to share the knowledge in question, but I didn't want to offend Miriam. She was my friend, after all. And Hans, however pretentious, was the son of this friend. I therefore promised that I would come, although I had to find a colleague on the national and foreign affairs editorial staff who would be willing to exchange my evening shift for his day shift.

The following Thursday when I arrived at Alex and Miriam's house, I had difficulty finding a parking place. Cars were parked everywhere, on the street and on the sidewalk. Half of the Jewish community was packed into the living room. At the very back of the room, Hans was handing out booklets that were lying in stacks on the closed piano lid. He had become taller and much thinner. Instead of the jeans he used to live in, he now wore a black suit that was too big for him. As I pushed my way toward Hans, I shook hands left and right, greeting friends.

"How are you?"

"Fine."

"How are you two?"

"Fine, fine."

It surprised me to encounter so much contentment, since we at the *Northern Daily* received such avalanches of bad news that we could have filled ten editions with it every day.

Finally I reached the piano.

"Hello, Hans, do you still remember me?" I said, extending my hand.

Shocked, as if I were contagious, he took a step back.

"I don't shake hands," he said. "Not with women."

He explained to me in detail why, as a pious Jew, he wasn't allowed to touch me. There was a gleam of triumph in his eyes. I knew that his indignation was a sham. Before me, at least twenty women had approached him with extended hand, and every time he had performed the same pantomime. He had recoiled from each of them and then bored them for some minutes while reciting sections from the Talmud and the Torah. I had no patience with it. While he was still talking to me, I resolutely turned my back on him.

In the kitchen I found Alex standing near a stack of boxes from a bakery. He was putting plastic cups on a tray. I gave him a kiss on his cheek.

"Have you been inside yet?" he said. "Have you spoken with the Great Guru yet?"

He laughed, but his expression was pained. For a moment I thought he was about to open his heart to me. Then he regained his self-control.

"Would you please help me with the pastry?" he asked. "Miriam went to the neighbors to borrow extra chairs. And I'm so clumsy today."

"Just tell me what I can do for you."

He pointed to a stack of plastic plates.

"There should be a ginger sweet roll on each plate."

I moved the pastry boxes from the overcrowded table to the kitchen counter, but there wasn't enough space there either. All the white plastic plates and forks went sailing through the air.

"Oh God," Alex said with a sigh. "There go the kosher plates." He looked at his watch. "It's too late to replace them," he said. "The stores are closed."

"Can't we just pick these up?" I suggested.

"Are you crazy? If Hans sees that, he'll kill us."

Helplessly we looked at the floor.

"Disposable dishes," said Alex. "The name is fitting."

For a moment we hesitated. Then, in common impulse, we both dove. In a panic, we grabbed at the plates. They were absolutely everywhere. We crawled around on all fours.

"Now for the forks!" I panted.

"Yes, the forks!" panted Alex.

At one point my forehead banged against his. Our eyes met. I saw the corners of his mouth tremble. We let ourselves fall backward, plates and all, and laughed till we cried.

"What's with you?" shouted Thérèse.

We lay at her feet on the kitchen floor and gasped for breath.

"The forks," I cried out, tears rolling down my face.

"If Hans saw this," roared Alex.

The tears rolled down our cheeks.

When the audience had finally consumed the coffee and ginger sweet rolls and when everyone was seated, Stella Silverberg made her entrance. Because she, like me, seldom came to the synagogue, I knew her only superficially. She was a real estate agent and dressed with an eccentric elegance. That evening she wore a chic gray suit and a small black hat with a veil. She was followed closely by a gangly young man, unknown to me, in a leotard with panther spots and a purple sweater. His long hair was tied in a ponytail. Like a zombie he walked behind Stella, his eyes staring straight ahead, as though he didn't see anyone in the room. Miriam got up to introduce herself to him, but Stella shook her head and whispered, loud enough for everyone to hear, "He doesn't shake hands."

I nudged Thérèse, who was sitting next to me.

"Could he be Orthodox, too?" I asked softly. "He certainly doesn't look it at all."

Deep in thought, Thérèse was startled. "What did you say?" she asked. "Who?"

"That boy in the spotted leotard."

"That's Stella's son," said Thérèse. "He's schizophrenic, not Orthodox. He's in treatment."

Meanwhile, standing in front of the piano, Hans was giving us a lecture. He spoke about the horrors of our time. Like a schoolmaster, he explained that war and famine, floods and other natural disasters, poverty and epidemics all were the writing on the wall, the labor pains of the Messiah's birth. We had reached rock bottom. But the choice was ours. We could hasten the coming of Mashiach by leading a God-fearing and pure life.

I only half listened to what he said. I kept looking at his lower jaw and the little grubby beard that grew there. With each frenzied movement of his mouth, the longest hairs of that little beard came in collision with the enormous Adam's apple jutting out of his thin neck. He didn't stand still for a moment. He skipped and tripped and swayed his head back and forth. I imagined myself back in my parents' house, where my father, as if in a trance, danced through the living room while he addressed the Brothers of Gibeon. I broke out in a sweat.

"I'm getting sick," I whispered to Thérèse.

"Who isn't?" said Isidore, who was sitting behind us.

Hans had picked up a booklet from the piano and was waving it around.

"Then the eyes of the blind will see again, and the ears of the deaf will hear again!" he shouted. "The lame will jump like the antelope, and the tongue of the dumb shall sing songs of joy!"

I got up from my seat and squeezed between the rows on my way to the door. In the kitchen, I drank a glass of water.

"Are you all right?" said Isidore, who had followed me.

I nodded.

Kindly, he patted me on the shoulder.

"All evening I've been wondering what I would do if I had a son like that," he said, "but I'm still not sure. I can't decide between kicking him to death and slow strangulation."

The cantor of our congregation also came in. He had caught Isidore's last words and sighed. "Strangulation seems drastic. That boy just needs a girl. He needs a good screw."

Isidore brought his fingers to his lips in a silencing gesture. "Watch out, mister," he said. "If you use language like that, the Messiah will never come!"

During his visit to Holland, Hans announced his desire to move to the Holy Land. In September he left for Israel, where he started his training for the rabbinate. Alex and Miriam boasted about his talents. Didn't they notice that a painful silence fell whenever they brought the conversation around to the subject of their son? Behind their backs, we wiped the floor with their darling boy.

"What a brat!" said Thérèse. "For a few years he's flipped through some books, and now he thinks he has a monopoly on wisdom."

"The way he stood there shouting," I said. "'Then the eyes of the blind will see again and the ears of the deaf will hear again!' It was just creepy."

"He was like Goebbels," said Isidore.

Rose, kindhearted and gullible as always, felt that we were unnecessarily gloomy.

"Other boys his age get addicted to alcohol and drugs," she said. "They go out at night and rob old people in the streets. Be glad that Hans reads the Torah. A bad thing doesn't come from a good thing."

But she couldn't convince us. We were long past the stage of dismissing Hans's fanaticism as an innocent symptom of adolescence.

It was 1992. A year earlier, during the Gulf War, the Chabad movement in Israel had caused quite a stir. After Saddam Hussein threatened to bombard the country with Iraqi poison-gas missiles, the Israelis barricaded themselves in their homes. Cracks and windows were sealed up with tape. Everyone, young and old, was given a gas mask. But while most of the population sat under the table, gas masks on, fearing for their lives, Chabadniks walked in the streets without masks. Their clairvoyant leader, Schneerson, had announced that these missiles wouldn't pose any danger. When events proved him right, the popularity of his movement increased. From Tel Aviv to Jerusalem, Chabad missionaries set to work. In tanks and vans, they rode through the country to call people to prayer. Hans joined them.

Meanwhile he kept bombarding me with propaganda leaflets. In December, I received another letter from him. In it he told me that he had gone on a pilgrimage to Hebron to pray at the cave of Machpela. In this cave, he wrote, Abraham and Sarah, Isaac and Rebecca, and Jacob and Leah were buried. Hebron was, according to Hans, the holiest place on earth, the be-all and end-all. Where did Adam and Eve live after their expulsion from paradise? In Hebron. Where did King David reside during the first seven years of his reign? In Hebron. And where, at the end of time, would the Messiah start his triumphal procession? In Hebron. It was outrageous that Palestinians had built a mosque on top of the cave of Machpela. Wasn't it written in black and white in scripture that Abraham had bought the cavern as well as the ground around it for four hundred pieces of silver? Hebron was a Jewish city. If the Palestinians did not want to recognize that, then they should just leave.

When I showed Thérèse the letter, she recognized the handwriting immediately.

"Do you save these?" she said. "I always tear mine up soon as they arrive."

"Then you receive letters from Hans, too?"

"Absolutely. But if you've read one, you've read them all. The message is always the same, just like the Evangelical Network."

"Does he rail against the Palestinians in his letters to you?"

"How would I know? I throw them in the garbage can unopened," said Thérèse.

"In this letter he calls the Palestinians mangy dogs and liars. He writes that if they don't disappear from Hebron voluntarily, they'll have to be driven away by force. That's not a very gentle attitude for a future rabbi."

Thérèse sighed. "The Palestinians in Hebron haven't been exactly gentle to the Jews. In 1929 they killed practically every Jew in the city."

"But *all* Palestinians didn't participate in this?"

"No," she acknowledged, "but hate has a long life."

"That hate is part of recent times," I said. "In the Middle Ages, Jews lived peacefully among Arabs. The caliphs were intelligent and tolerant hosts. And the Jews, in turn, were grateful guests. Not only did they make Arabic their spoken language, but they also wrote their books about geometry, astronomy, and medicine—to name a few—in Arabic."

"Still they were second-class citizens. They had to wear special clothing and pay high taxes."

"Yes, but no Arab stood in the way of their development. Under Arab rule they flowered; under Arab rule they felt at home."

"They weren't allowed to build synagogues."

"That's beside the point. They weren't persecuted. They were respected in science, literature, commerce. And they reached high positions at court."

Thérèse shrugged her shoulders.

"Palace Jews," she said. "You had those in the Christian world as well."

"In the Christian world, palace Jews were the exception that proved the rule. And the rule was that Jews were slaughtered by the Crusaders. The rule was that Jews were roasted over fires by the Cossacks. Their lives were in jeopardy. From one day to the next they could be banished or forced to live in stinking ghettos, because the king wanted to fill his treasury or because the queen was bothered by her corns."

Thérèse laughed, but I was serious.

"Medieval Arabs had more respect for Jews than twentieth-century Europeans did. Until recently the greatest Jewish thinkers were dragged through the mud. In Germany in 1933, an anti-Semitic book with photographs of Jews was published. Its title was *Juden sehen dich an.* Among others, there was a photo of Albert Einstein with the caption 'Not yet hanged.'"

"Even Freud was driven away." Thérèse nodded. "He couldn't stand the harassment. House searches by the Gestapo, storm troopers all over the place. But he had to ransom himself, and he wasn't allowed to leave Vienna until he had paid an enormous sum of money."

"In the Arab caliphate, insulting a Jewish scholar was unthinkable," I said. "They had a deep respect for knowledge, whether held by Muslims, Jews, or others."

Thérèse poured some hot chocolate. We were sitting by the potbellied stove in her studio while the rain beat against the windows.

"So you think that Jews and Arabs should reconcile," she said.

"I don't know whether we've ever been brothers, and I doubt that we'll ever become brothers. But if you accept the Torah literally, then the Arabs are the closest relatives we have, our first cousins. Shouldn't we draw conclusions from that?"

"You're forgetting," said Thérèse, "that many Jews in Israel are refugees from Morocco, Tunisia, Libya, Iraq, and Iran. They lived there for hundreds of years, but they were treated like animals by those tolerant Arabs of yours. And now they have to embrace these same Arabs? You can't expect the impossible."

"Is it really so impossible? You live among people who have

worse things on their conscience than that. While half of them tried to murder you, the other half looked on indifferently. They dragged you to the other end of the world, where they raped your mother, gassed your father, threw your brothers and sisters into a pit, starved your aunts to death, and shot your uncles in the back of the head. There's no cruelty too appalling for them not to have committed. And you came back to these people. Every day you walk among them on the street, and you say good morning, please, and thank-you to them."

"Yes, but you can't dwell on it. You lick your wounds, you straighten your back, and you go on with life."

"If that's possible," I said, "shouldn't it be much simpler to live in peace with the Palestinians?"

The longer Hans lived in Israel, the more militant his letters became. Finally he had a suitable target for his frustrations. His parents, at whom he had originally aimed his anger, had barely resisted him. In the Palestinians he found enemies of stature. Like a gift from heaven, their existence legitimatized his rage, the rage of a toddler who wants to open the door but who is too small to reach the doorknob, and it gave this rage an adult air. Finally, the world would take him seriously. In his letters, which he now wrote on the computer, the better to send out more at once, he called the Palestinians sons of bitches and worms, syphilitics, murderers, and fascists.

***

One afternoon Miriam came to my door by bicycle. Her blond curls were windblown, and her forehead had frown lines that I'd never seen before.

"Do you have a minute?" she asked.

She lowered her eyes; she hadn't been in touch for months. Even in the synagogue she had avoided me.

I laughed.

"What is it?"

"Nothing. I suddenly remembered the first time that you rang my bell. You invited me for a Jewish evening."

She nodded. "And you asked what in the world you'd be doing there."

"You said that it would be very nice."

"But I hadn't even finished pouring coffee and passing the cookies when Rose and Isidore started in about concentration camps."

We roared with laughter.

"You had just moved," I said, "and boxes were piled everywhere. You were very pregnant, and a month later Hans was born."

Her face became somber.

"Hans," she sighed, "Hans."

While we were walking to the living room, she told me that he'd left for Hebron.

"To *stay* there," she emphasized. "He's left Jerusalem and is planning to abandon his education. We don't even know his new address; we have only a post office box number. But he can't be living in a post office box."

"What does he want to do in Hebron?"

"Pray, fast, wait. He says the Messiah is coming."

"How does he figure that?"

"He's calculated it."

"Then I hope he's better at counting than at spelling. The letters he sends me are full of mistakes."

"He's not a language genius," admitted Miriam. "But he does have a vast knowledge of Jewish issues."

"In that case he should know that it isn't kosher to predict when the Messiah is coming. The Talmud expressly advises against it."

Miriam shrugged her shoulders.

"The greatest Talmudists have made predictions," she said. "Rashi, Nachmanides, and so on."

"That only proves that even the greatest Talmudists have done stupid things."

"According to Hans, the Messiah should be landing shortly, in the cave of Machpela."

"Landing? Is he coming by spaceship?"

"It is written that he will descend."

"So much is written. It says that he will descend, and it says that he will rise from among us. It says that God will send him when the time is ripe, and it says that God will hasten his coming. It says that redemption will come when we have bettered our lives, and it says that that won't happen until we have sunk to the deepest possible depravity. And there's much more that can't be reconciled. In the Talmud all these contradictions are cleverly balanced so that no one can complain afterward that he was fooled."

"So you think that all this is fraud?"

"The stories about the Messiah are so ambiguous and so enigmatic that they make it quite possible for us to deceive *ourselves*. Has redemption not yet come because we live in sin? Or are we not sinful enough? It's a mystery to me."

"Hans says that many messiahs have been born and have died. They were ready to redeem the world, but the world wasn't ready for them."

"Hans says, Hans says," I repeated impatiently. "It is indeed asserted that a messiah lives in every generation. But somewhere else it says that the Messiah is an exceptional individual who will overshadow all preceding prophets, someone who will surpass Solomon in wisdom and be greater than Moses."

Offended, Miriam averted her eyes. When she looked at me again, there was mistrust in her glance.

"Do you actually believe in the Messiah?" she asked.

"I don't know what to believe."

"Do you long for his coming?"

"He'll appear sooner or later, but I'm not looking forward to it."

"What do you mean?"

"I'm afraid that we can't expect much good from Hans's Messiah. He's a tyrant of the worst kind. Anyone he doesn't like immediately, he hurls into the sea of fire. Anyone who doesn't cheerfully beat his machine gun into a plowshare gets the death penalty. Even Stalin didn't finish off his victims that thoroughly. Once in a while, he would send someone to Siberia to cut down trees."

"What do you expect?" said Miriam. "You can't redeem the world if you don't eradicate evil."

"Has the thought ever occurred to you," I said, "that the world *cannot* be saved? If people could stop bashing in each other's brains, why haven't they done so? Nothing is preventing them from making a promising start today, or perhaps tomorrow, when they come home from work."

"They can do it, but not without help. That's exactly why they need the Messiah."

"Nonsense," I said. "The Christians have had their Messiah for almost two thousand years, and it hasn't gotten them anywhere."

Miriam looked put out.

"If you don't believe in the coming of the Messiah, then you place yourself outside Judaism," she said. "If you don't long for his coming, then you basically reject the whole Torah. That's what Hans says."

"Fortunately I don't depend on Hans for my salvation," I said angrily.

"What do you mean?"

"Yesterday he didn't know the difference between Genesis and a hole in the ground, but today he considers himself the greatest scriptural scholar of all time. And you go along with that. You even invite your best friends to let themselves be threatened by him with hell and damnation."

"Do you mean the lecture he gave? You're the only one who was upset by it."

"Everyone was upset by it; everyone thinks that Hans is a conceited pain in the ass who's in urgent need of a spanking. But I'm one of the few who will say so."

"Alex and I also don't agree with all his opinions," said Miriam stiffly, "but we're impressed with his perseverance and his enthusiasm. In the past he would run after a soccer ball all day long. His interest for Judaism has given direction to his life."

"That's wonderful," I said, "but it's no reason for him to force others to change their lives in that direction. That goes for you, too. I don't like being cross-examined by you!"

"Cross-examined?"

"Do I believe in the coming of the Messiah? Do I secretly doubt the salvation of humanity? Am I a good Jew? Who should decide that? You, who make Judaism into a theatrical performance? Don't make me laugh."

Miriam stood up.

"My God, what a bitch!" she said, putting on her coat. "I knew it all along, but Alex kept insisting that I was imagining it. You never did anything for the Jewish community. You watched while we worked like mad to get people together, to find a rabbi and a cantor, to organize prayer services. You never lifted a finger. No wonder you hate Hans. He embodies everything that you're not. He doesn't avoid responsibility—he puts himself at the service of others. He lives totally in the spirit of the Torah."

She stalked out of the room, but I followed her.

"He sends letters in which he calls Palestinians worms and syphilitics," I said to her back. "He'd prefer to run them out of Israel today. Is that in the spirit of the Torah? If only he'd stayed on the soccer field, where he'd do considerably less harm."

Miriam trembled with rage. "At least he dares to believe in something," she said. "And he makes no secret of it. Yes, he's sure of what he's doing. But should you reproach him for his conviction just because you yourself doubt everything?"

She was already outside and was angrily fiddling with her bicycle lock.

"Do you know why the Talmud says that we're not permitted to make predictions about the coming of the Messiah?" I said, standing in the doorway. "Because if he doesn't come when we expect him, we might despair. And desperate people are capable of the most awful things."

She didn't react. Judging me unworthy of another glance, she got on her bicycle and rode off, disappearing around the corner.

During the following months I was quite busy. In May, the *Northern Daily* moved to a new building on the outskirts of Groningen. And when I had finally found my niche there, I was transferred from the national and foreign affairs editorial staff to the city desk. Soon I discovered that I knew far too little about municipal politics in general and about those of Groningen in particular. The city turned out to be a world unto itself, with its own balance of power and its own conflicts of interest. Before I'd done mainly work in the office, but now I was almost constantly on the move. At the city desk there was no day or night shift; all the journalists were on duty from early morning until late at night. In my spare time I studied old transcripts of municipal council meetings and other files in order to make up for my lack of factual information. I hardly had time for anything but work.

Hans kept sending me letters and flyers, but following Thérèse's example I now threw each envelope with its cramped writing into the wastebasket unopened. I did this without qualm. But I found it much more difficult to ignore his parents. Since our quarrel, Miriam hadn't called me. Nor did I do anything to break the icy silence. Because I didn't know what else to do, I stopped going to gatherings of the Jewish community. I even avoided the company of Rose, Isidore, and Thérèse. Meanwhile I felt guiltier all the time. Why had I felt compelled to tell Miriam the truth? Why had I put our friendship on the line? Wasn't friendship more important than any truth?

One evening in August I got a call from my mother. I recognized her voice, but the connection was bad. There was an ominous whistling in the phone, as if she were standing on the polar ice cap in a snowstorm that was about to blow her away.

"The Eternal has given and the Eternal has taken away," I heard her say. "The name of the Eternal be praised."

Was she doing missionary work among the polar bears?

"Is it you, Mameh?"

"You don't need to shout so," she said. "I hear you fine."

"Yes, but I can barely understand you."

"Your father is dead. His heart stopped. It happened while he was saying his morning prayer. He suddenly fell forward to the floor and he stopped moving."

What did she mean, "he stopped moving"? I saw my father before me again, the way he became entranced during the meetings of the Brothers of Gibeon. The way he shook and danced, swept away by the sound of his own voice. He hadn't stood still for a moment, but had he ever really budged? With his petrified thoughts he had been as unyielding as a pillar of salt.

I tried my very best to feel something, but I didn't succeed. My mother was calm, too. She gave the impression that she didn't have to control any sorrow.

"He died as he lived," she said matter-of-factly. "In the hands of the Almighty."

She was right; he had been a tool in the hands of his supposed Creator. As long as I'd known him, he had blindly obeyed strict laws. Day in and day out, he'd sat bent over scripture without the slightest feeling for the characters who were portrayed in it and without the least understanding for the flaws that they displayed. Even the greatest heroes of Jewish history had deviated from the right path, even the staunchest patriarchs and the bravest kings had known moments of weakness. Cunning and deception, murder and carnage, love and lust: nothing human was foreign to them because they were involved in life. My father, in his pride, had placed himself above them and outside the world. Yes, he had been virtuous. But how useful was the virtue of someone who had never exposed himself to any temptation whatsoever?

I promised that I'd come to the funeral, although I was obligated to no one—especially not to the deceased himself, who had declared me dead years ago and who had never wavered from that decision.

The next day at the crack of dawn I left for Putte, near the border of Belgium. There, south of Bergen op Zoom, religious Jews have been buried for generations, not out of preference but because they can't get a suitable resting place in their own country. Jewish law prescribes that the dead remain untouched until the Messiah raises them from the dust on Judgment Day. But that's too long for the Belgians, who refuse to contribute their fine soil for that. According to Belgian law, a grave must be cleared by the end of one hundred years. This is why Jews who won't let wild horses kick them out of Belgium while they're still alive nonetheless are forced to emigrate after death. My father was such a posthumous emigrant.

When I arrived at the cemetery, it was black with hats and white with beards. About five hundred people had gathered to pay their last respects to my father. The period of mourning for the destruction of the Temple had just passed. Those present, who for days had listened to the traditional lamentations in a dimly lit synagogue, were quietly waiting for the ceremony to start. With unwilling steps I proceeded into the crowd. It took a while before I found my mother. She was much older and grayer than I remembered.

"I no longer recognize you," I said in Yiddish.

"In twenty years quite a few wrinkles have been added," she answered stiffly.

Like total strangers we faced each other.

"Did Tateh ever talk about me?" I asked it in a muffled voice, almost whispering.

"*Der Tateh?*" She looked at me searchingly. "About you?"

"He must have said something; he must have mentioned my name at least once?"

I searched her face for a hint of pity. But her eyes remained cold as ice.

"Why would he?"

"Maybe he missed me."

"If that was the case, he never let on."

"Never at all?"

"You can't blame him. You have only yourself to thank for all this."

"He sprinkled ashes on his head. He cast me out."

"You could have written a letter. You could have done so many things; you could have talked with him."

"Talk, with him? It was impossible to talk with him."

"You haven't changed," she said bitterly. "You think only about yourself. Did you come here to drag your father through the mud? Go right ahead. He can't defend himself now."

At that moment, the president of the funeral society began the prayer.

"He, the Rock, his work is perfect. He is just and fair. Is he not your Father who created you? Did he not make you and give you your destiny?"

The crowd began to sway back and forth and murmur. In its motion, my mother was pushed forward to where the coffin with my father in it was lifted mysteriously, as though floating. Then the procession started moving.

I walked at the rear, blinded by tears, while from hundreds of mouths resounded the old psalm: "His angels will protect you, wherever you go. They will carry you on their hands, so that your foot will not stumble on a rock." Over and over the casket was set down reverentially, and over and over new bearers pushed forward to lift it. When they finally lowered their burden into the earth, I turned around. The path seemed made of foam rubber. With the unsteady steps of a moon traveler, I left the mourners farther and farther behind until even their many-voiced prayers were out of hearing.

On the way back to Groningen I cried in anger. Apparently my father had succeeded in banishing me not only from his house but also from his thoughts. Me, the daughter on whom, for lack of a son, he had pinned his hopes, the daughter whom he had educated as though she had been born to be a rabbi. For years I had been subjected to his rigid discipline. While other girls of my age still played with dolls, I had had to learn Hebrew and read the Torah under his watchful eye. But when I finally took my destiny into my own hands, he crossed out my name from the Book of Life. And since that time I'd never been completely sure of my existence.

Angrily, I pushed down on the gas pedal. Through the windshield I looked up at the sun. Could it possibly revolve around the earth anyway, without anyone noticing, just because my father had willed it?

I had a headache by the time I got home. I closed the curtains and fell into a short but deep sleep on the sofa in the living room. I awoke in the early evening. The pain had retreated to behind my eyes, but the throbbing increased every time I thought of the funeral and of my mother's brusqueness. To distract myself, I turned on the television.

A documentary about the black rhinoceros in Zimbabwe was on. A biologist was reporting that the animal was still being hunted for its horn, which, when ground to powder, was supposed to increase male potency. Druggists, quacks, and shamans sold the stuff for exorbitant prices. To prevent the last remaining eighteen rhinos from being sacrificed to this superstition, conservationists had decided to remove their horns. From a small airplane the animals were shot with a dose of anesthesia. Then someone used a Black and Decker saw to remove the horn just above the root. The shrill sound of the saw cut through me like a knife, and I turned my eyes away. When I looked again, one of the animals had regained consciousness. Drowsily he was scrambling to his feet. His horn lay next to him on the ground. On his head a dark stump remained. On both sides of it his small eyes blinked in surprise at a hornless horizon.

I quickly switched to another channel. There the news was in full swing. Excited men with hats and side curls were moving on the screen. For a moment I expected to see my father's coffin. But this wasn't Putte, this was Israel.

In the streets of Hebron, fierce clashes broke out today between Jewish settlers and Palestinians. One of the settlers suddenly started shooting. A sixteen-year-old Palestinian was hit by three bullets and died on the way to the hospital. The perpetrator, a twenty-one-year-old Jew, originally from Holland, was overpowered by Israeli soldiers. He said that he had been acting according to orders from God. . . .

That was Hans, without a doubt! For a few seconds his face filled the screen. Around his mouth hovered the same triumphant smile I saw when he refused to shake my hand in his parents' house.

Hebron on the occupied West Bank of the Jordan River has for years been the scene of battles between Palestinian and Jewish extremists. The cause of the continually flaring hostilities is the cave of Machpela, where, according to tradition, Abraham, forefather of the Jews as well as the Muslims, is buried. Both groups consider this place the cradle of their culture and demand possession of the grave for themselves.

Several residents of the small Jewish quarter of Hebron spoke. Behind them rose the dramatic barbed-wire barricade that they had built to fence themselves off from the outside world. They declared that no Jew in Hebron was safe from the hatred of the Palestinians. Some called the murder a sad but unavoidable chance occurrence. Others openly declared their approval or admiration for Hans's act. According to them he had given the Palestinians what they deserved, an eye for an eye, a tooth for a tooth. One of them pulled a pistol from his pants pocket under the fringes of his prayer shirt and waved it angrily in front of the camera. "You don't think that we can go out into the street unarmed, do you?" he shouted stridently. "This is the jungle, sir! We have been thrown into the lions' den, like Daniel. We are here among wild animals!"

I got up and walked around the house like a sleepwalker, from the living room to the kitchen and back again. As I went, I did meaningless things as if in a trance: I took a magazine from the table and put it back again in the same place, I opened a drawer and pushed it shut again. My headache was forgotten; I was now overcome by a feeling of acute panic that numbed all of my senses.

After a while I dialed Thérèse's telephone number, but no one answered.

I had better luck with Isidore and Rose.

"Yes," Isidore said with a sigh, "we've also seen it."

"Maybe it wasn't Hans," I said. "Maybe it was just someone who looked exactly like him."

"No, it definitely was Hans. Thérèse has already spoken to Alex and Miriam on the phone. We're going over there. Rose and I were just about to leave."

"Do you think that I could go there, too?" I said hesitatingly.

"That all depends," Isidore said sharply. "If you feel compelled to say that Hans should have stayed on the soccer field, then please don't come. Alex and Miriam can figure that out by themselves. They don't need you for that."

Apparently Miriam had told him all about our confrontation.

"It's easy to laugh at others' mistakes," he said. "After the camp, Rose could no longer have children. We've always thought that was terrible. But secretly I sometimes think that we should be glad about it. I don't know what I would have done if Hans were *my* son. Would I have had a terrible fight with him? Would I have kicked him out of the house? And would that have helped? I'm in the fortunate position of not having had to make that decision."

"Do you think Miriam would like to see me?" I asked.

"I don't know," said Isidore. "It wouldn't surprise me if she didn't feel like it on an evening like this. But that isn't the point, is it? The question is whether you think it's worth giving it a try."

"I'd like to try," I said.

"Then we'll meet you there," said Isidore, "in fifteen minutes."

In the car I was hot with shame. Isidore was right. What did we know about having children and enduring lifelong worries about them? I remember years ago, when Hans was still a toddler, how Miriam had told me that she couldn't sleep at night because she was afraid that something would happen to him. With eyes wide open and ears alert, she lay in the dark ready to jump up at the slightest sound and attack any danger whatsoever. She wasn't afraid even of the devil.

Had my mother in the distant past watched over me as passionately? Perhaps, perhaps. But not after my eighteenth birthday. Then, because my father had cast me out and because the book of Leviticus justified it, I no longer played a role in her life.

Miriam and Alex, on the other hand, had continued to love their son against their better judgment. The further he had distanced himself from them, the closer they had locked him in their hearts. The more peculiarly he started behaving, the more fiercely they defended him to others. They had braved their own doubts and the ridicule of half the world. For that you needed courage, the kind of courage that my parents had lacked.

Thérèse opened the door after I rang the bell. She gave me a quick kiss, as though we'd seen each other only the day before. Nervously I followed her to the enclosed porch, where Alex, Miriam, Isidore, and Rose were sitting.

"What you need," I heard Isidore say, "is the advice of a specialist. Not just any lawyer, but a very good one."

"We'll find one," said Alex. "But we didn't hear until five o'clock this afternoon. We haven't been able to do much yet."

No one looked surprised when I came in. Isidore pushed up a chair and I was automatically, almost casually, included in the conversation.

"Do you think that they know yet at the paper?" Alex asked me.

"I didn't go to work today," I said, "but I can find out tomorrow."

"If there's anything I'm not in the mood for," Miriam said, "it's having journalists all over the house." She placed her hand on mine for a minute. "Except for you, of course," she said.

Alex started to cry. The tears streamed down his cheeks and he did nothing to stop them. It was as if he didn't notice. He sat at the table, motionless, while his face kept getting wetter.

"We should never have let him go to Hebron," Miriam said softly. "All the lunatics from Israel are concentrated there. Of course they used him. It's not like Hans to walk around with a pistol, let alone shoot it. When he was small, I once took him along to the veterinarian. Yupi's claws needed to be cut, but that man cut too close and one started bleeding. Hans began to sob terribly. He never could stand to see blood."

"That was the blood of a parrot," said Alex somberly. "He seems to have less difficulty with the blood of Palestinians."

"Perhaps that boy provoked him. You don't know," said Miriam.

"But how?" said Alex. "He didn't have a weapon; they emptied his pockets and found nothing, not even a knife."

"You don't know," repeated Miriam.

"We *do* know," shouted Alex. "Hans confessed. And a whole crowd of witnesses was standing right there."

"It's hard to believe," mumbled Miriam. "The day before yesterday he called and asked if I would buy socks for him. 'The socks here are of such bad quality,' he said, 'after a week they've got holes.'"

"And he's even proud of it!" said Alex, covering his eyes with his hands. "He seems to have said that he wants to clear the way for the Messiah. And I can believe it. For months we've been getting the craziest letters from him."

"Yes," said Miriam. "He had dreams in which Isaiah and Jeremiah appeared to him."

"They gave him messages and orders," said Alex. "He had to erase the name of Amalek from under the heavens. That sort of thing. He felt called to action; he felt like a hero."

Miriam nodded.

"He was totally confused. I even sent him a small bottle of valerian drops."

"It all started with Antwerp," said Alex. "I should never have let him leave the local school. But I was busy. I had just started that new project and was working sixteen hours a day. Hans was the least of my worries. The very least."

Isidore tried to console him.

"You're not responsible," he said.

"Don't say that!" said Alex. "I'm his father. If I'm not responsible, then who is?"

"Even Hans isn't responsible," said Isidore. "Someone who thinks that he gets orders from Isaiah and Jeremiah, someone like that can't be held accountable. He needs to see a psychiatrist."

After this a deep silence fell, during which Thérèse got up to pour coffee.

When, a moment later, she pulled shortbread out of her bag, Isidore started laughing.

"Women!" he said. "A disaster happens and what do they do? They think of *shortbread.*"

"A disaster with shortbread is easier to bear than a disaster without," contended Thérèse while cutting the shortbread into pieces.

"That reminds me of when I was young," said Rose. "Whenever disturbances against the Jews broke out in our village, my mother brought the most delicious things out from the cellar. Then we would sit, the shutters closed, and eat the whole supply of canned fruit, as if it were a holiday. 'Hurry up,' my mother would say, 'or do you want the anti-Semites to take it with them?' Because during those disturbances, Jewish homes would be completely ransacked."

"All right then, let's do it," Miriam said with a sigh as she was handed a wedge of shortbread. "I haven't had a bite to eat yet."

"Please give me two pieces," said Alex. "I can't bear the thought of leaving even a crumb for the anti-Semites."

***

Hans was charged with murder. He was sentenced to three years in prison and two years of compulsory psychiatric treatment. Alex and Miriam visit him in Jerusalem as often as they can manage.

Not long ago Hans sent me a letter from prison. "The end is coming," he wrote, "the end over the four corners of the land. The day is near. Blow the trumpet and be ready."

With some regularity I give his parents packages to take along to him. They contain chewing gum and socks and, if it works out, the newest *Suske and Wiske* comic book.

I've offered my translation of the poems of Samuel Ha-Nagid to several literary magazines, but there's no interest in them. Meanwhile I'm translating the poetry of Moses Ibn Ezra. He too was a Jew who lived in medieval Spain. He too fought on the Islamic side against the Christian monarchs. Twice he witnessed the destruction of Granada, and twice his heart was broken.

It doesn't seem likely that my translations will ever appear in print. But that doesn't matter very much. Through them I'm able to fulfill the holiest of all Jewish commandments, the commandment to keep on learning.

TRANSLATED FROM THE DUTCH
BY JEANNETTE K. RINGOLD

REINVENTION

On My Great-Grandfather, My Grandfather, My Father, and Me

Barbara Honigmann

Barbara Honigmann was born in 1949 in East Berlin, where she stud-
ied theater before beginning her career as a dramaturge and theater di-
rector. Though she has been writing since 1975, she did not begin to pub-
lish until after moving to Strasbourg, France, with her family in 1984.
Her prose works include Roman von einem Kinde (Novel about a
Child, *1986*), Eine Liebe aus Nichts (*1991; translated as* A Love
Made out of Nothing, *2003*), Soharas Reise (*1996; translated as*
Zohara's Journey, *2003*), *and* Alles, alles Liebe (With All My
Love, *2000*). *She has also published several collections of essays and is*
an acclaimed painter. Honigmann has received many literary prizes,
among them the prestigious Kleist Preis and, in 2004, the Koret Jewish
Book Award.

 Honigmann explains her ambivalent attitude toward the term "Ger-
man Jewish writer": "I at times associate a certain pride with it, and if
only to respond to Gershom Scholem's statement about the illusion of a
'German Jewish symbiosis.' And yet, never again self-denial, never
again abandonment. Never again a love affair with the Germans. My
discomfort with the classification as a German Jewish writer also sprung
from the fear of being perceived too little as a writer (and artist) and
rather only as a Jew. The discomfort is further increased by an exagger-
ated and extraliterary interest in my life which has been stamped as 'Or-
thodox,' in which I feel the shiver and the attraction of the voyeur.
Instead of questions relating to my work, I often have to answer ques-
tions about my reconciliation with religion and halacha. I have slowly

lost patience and feel more and more like answering: 'Okay, I am Or-
thodox, so what?'"

✷

Sometimes we ride our bicycles down to the Rhine; it is, after
all, only fifteen minutes from our house. There is a park there and
a path along the river. On the German side one can even walk or
bike all the way up it to Basel, but on the French side it gets lost
in a steppe in front of an industrial plant, and we are, after all,
on the French side. Shortly before reaching the steppe, we sat
down on a bench and looked across the river; over there is Germany. I said to Peter, "Now we don't really know anymore where
we belong"; but Peter answered, "That isn't really important to
me. We simply belong at our writing desks."

The trees rustle because a wind is blowing. On the bench beside us sits another family; their children are playing ball. The
wind carries the ball away and it falls at our feet; we throw it
back and the child throws it again to us, and it goes on like this
for a while, and then we are talking, first to the child and then
with its parents. They are Turks. They used to be in Germany;
now they have a shop in Strasbourg, not too far from us. We
really must go there sometime.

They must have recognized us as Jews from Peter's beard and
cap, and they ask us if we also have a shop.

"No, we don't have one," we say. This amazes them, because
most Jews do own shops—watch shops, jewelry shops, and fabric shops. But we were doing well?

"Yes, we are doing well, quite well. One really couldn't claim
otherwise, yes, thank you."

Then they ask, "And tell us, how did you do it, with the exile? How did you manage to do so well, to get such good positions, even wealth and power?" We look at each other, Peter and
I. Wealth? Power? Positions? Well off?

My great-grandfather, David Honigmann, was the secretary-
general of the Silesian railway. He had learned German as a

fourteen-year-old through Moses Mendelssohn's translation of
the Bible, so he says in the memoirs of his childhood and youth;
the language he spoke prior to this he called "the dialect" and
most likely meant Yiddish. His whole life long, he battled for
the emancipation of the Jews in Prussia, and since he received so
much support from the Liberals in this battle, he himself became
a Liberal, a Democrat, and a member of the German Progressive
Party (Deutsche Fortschrittspartei). He also participated in the
Revolution of 1848. I once received a letter from Jerusalem in-
quiring whether I was a descendant of David Honigmann, the
Democrat from the Revolution of '48, and I responded with
pride, "Yes, that's me."

My great-grandfather also wanted to carry the new ideas over
into Judaism itself, whose petrified, authoritative condition he
still remembered with terror from his childhood; he belonged to
those who invented and founded Reform Judaism.

He was also a writer, a German writer; he wrote novels and
novellas in a rather conventional style. He was therefore no Heine
or Börne, or even a Berthold Auerbach, with whom he was close
friends. He was close friends with absolutely everybody who at
the time had such a great desire for German culture. He wrote for
the periodical *Der Israelit* (*The Israelite*); he polemicized against
the anti-Semitic, conservative parties and worked as an attorney
on laws and regulations that eventually enabled Jews to enter
into Prussian society and achieve equality. His obituary states
that he had been a champion of inner and outer emancipation:
"He fearlessly mounted the barricades whenever Prussian Jews
were threatened or treated with injustice. He died a loyal Jew, a
good German, and an honest man."[1]

His son Georg Gabriel, my grandfather, decided, however, to
leave Judaism completely and enter into German society; he assimilated himself before complete emancipation was attained,
for he still had to wait quite a while for his appointment as a full
professor. He served science—not exactly its established central
disciplines, like many of his Jewish colleagues, but rather in new
areas, on the margins, in his case homeopathy and medical his-

tory.[2] At the University of Gießen, the holder of the Chair of
Medical History still sits today beneath the portrait of the
founder of this chair: namely, my grandfather. He was, of course,
also the editor of the periodical, whose name, to be sure, was no
longer *Der Israelit* but rather *Hippokrates* and in which he tried to
renew the field of medicine in every sense of the word.[3]

He offered the German fatherland his firstborn son, Heinrich,
my father's only brother, as a sacrifice. Heinrich fell in September of 1918 as an ensign of Regiment 113 of the Fifth Baden In-
fantry; even sixty years later my father knew the regiment number by heart. It was around here somewhere, in France, not far
from where I now live. Touring the Vosges on Sundays, we have
often made hair-raising discoveries. Some of the mountains are
sown with graves. At first one doesn't notice, for there are so
many pieces of red sandstone lying about, from which the Strasbourg Cathedral is built. It is only when one looks closely or
wants to sit down for a picnic precisely upon such a piece of stone
that one discovers the inscriptions with no names, only things like
"Two French Soldiers," "Eight German Soldiers," "Six French-
men," "Two Germans," and the regiment numbers underneath.
It is like this all the way to the summit; they lie there every few
feet, as if the dead men must constantly climb up the mountain,
metamorphosed into red stone. My father's name was also Georg,
like his father, but in full it was Georg Friedrich Wolfgang. One
can readily see in these forenames that there was nothing left of
Judaism, not even a second or third given name. He received his
doctorate too, of course, in accordance with the well-known joke,
"What is the most common Jewish first name in Germany? Doctor!" My father no longer had to leave Judaism; it was already
thoroughly removed from him and foreign to him. He had perhaps even almost "forgotten" it and actually believed that Germany was his homeland and that he himself was a German.

This belief was shattered for him when he had to flee the German homeland to foreign countries and hide, but even there the
Germans continued to look for Jews, the way cannibals look for
human flesh. My father offered an ironic modification of the say-

ing from the Jewish Haskalah about being at home a Jew and on the street a person: "At home a person and on the street a Jew." When he returned after the war, nobody even wanted to know anymore what a Jew was, and he was asked on the street time and time again if he was a Turk, a Greek, or an Italian. He joined the political movement that promised him "equality and fraternity" (liberty was a lesser priority), that purported not to know any race divisions, only class divisions, and that simply wanted to eliminate the "Jewish question" as a concept: Communism. Like his father and grandfather, he edited newspapers. He also wrote books, as they did, but these were biographies of people who had the least in common with him and who did not interest him at all, and he published them with a press that he despised due to its other publications.[4]

The literary efforts of my father had nothing of the euphoria, not even the illusions, with which his forefathers wished to inscribe themselves into German culture. It was submission to the party, self-denial of his Jewishness and of his bourgeois heritage. At home there remained only irony and distance, which constituted merely another expression of his desperation. In a journal from the early years after the war, which I read after his death, I found the entry: "Was at the circus tonight. Went home sad, for I have absolutely no idea where I am. Like the Italian who just performed there and actually comes from Russia. Just as much an Italian as I am."[5]

My great-grandfather, my grandfather, and my father dreamed of being "at home" in the German culture; they desired it, reached out for it, and stretched and contorted themselves unbelievably in order to unite themselves with it. Instead of unification, they mostly experienced denial and repulsion, and my father was given the privilege of witnessing the final destruction of German Jewish history with his own eyes.

And I, the great-granddaughter of the fearless champion, now stood there at a loss, a rather fearful descendant. After some consideration and observation, I thought to myself that I would just let it all go—the championing of causes and throwing oneself into things. I prefer to separate myself, I decided, detach myself, remain at the margin, in the distance. It would be best to live in another country, without embarrassment, only as a neighbor to the Germans. That would already be quite a lot.

I moved to Strasbourg. There I live on the edge of the inner city, three blocks beyond the border, as if my courage had reached no farther.

When I came to that other country, even if it was only three blocks beyond the border, I also began to write—or, shall we say, "really" to write, like my great-grandfather, my grandfather, and my father. I wrote, of course, in German, like them, and published with German presses. That was, then, already a return, and I had scarcely left. But perhaps writing was also something like homesickness and an assurance that we really did belong together, Germany and I, that we, as they say, could not get away from each other, especially not now, after everything that had happened, that, as Dan Diner so correctly remarked, the so-called German Jewish symbiosis perhaps did not actually come into being until Auschwitz.[6] My writing had, in effect, come from a more or less fortuitous separation, just as couples write each other love letters at the very beginning of their infatuation and then not again until their breakup. I had even experienced such a thing myself, when I still lived in Berlin: I had written a few plays there and had composed them after I had left the theater for good, because I had understood that my profession could never be in the theater and that the world of the theater simply could never be my world. I wrote these plays, so to say, as a farewell, so that something would nevertheless remain between us, between the theater and myself, so that not all the bridges would be burned.

I wanted to present myself completely differently than my great-grandfather, my grandfather, and my father, and now I saw myself, just like them, speaking again to the Other, hoping to be heard, perhaps even to be understood, calling to him, "Look at me! Listen to me, at least for five minutes." When I really think about it, the shortness of my texts has to do with the fear that people would stop listening to me if I spoke longer, that I only have a short time frame.

I understood that writing means being separated and is very similar to exile and that it is in this sense perhaps true that being a writer and being a Jew are similar as well, in the way they are dependent upon the Other when they speak to him, more or less despairingly. It is true of both that approaching the Other too closely is dangerous for them and that agreeing with him too completely will bring about their downfall.

In contrast to the beliefs of my great-grandfather, my grandfather, and my father, I no longer believe that one can be released early from exile, "on good behavior," so to speak. This reminds me of how a friend of mine came back from Israel recently and said she hadn't felt right there at all and hadn't the slightest idea why. My friend comes from Libya and, after the expulsion of the Jews, lived in Rome before marrying and coming to Strasbourg. Later she found an explanation: she had not felt right in Israel simply because there had been no Other there, in relation to which we had always lived. "I was completely lost, being always among my own kind," she said.

When I was a child, it was said that I had the Jewish knack. That was said of me by my parents, who were also Jews and had the knack of hiding their Jewishness whenever possible. To forget it, however, was no longer a possibility for them. They lived among the Other, like the Marranos, conforming on the outside while clinging on the inside to the indefinable je ne sais quoi of Judaism.[7]

At home they spoke only about "it"; outside, though, they never spoke about "it." And when others spoke about the war, Silesia, East Prussia, Treck, the bombardments of German cities, and the evil deeds of the Red Army, they were silent. I often thought: Why does everybody get to tell his or her story, and only we are not allowed to tell ours? At that time I did not yet know that it indeed took twenty years for this generation of survivors to begin to talk, twenty years until others could listen to them, and that it took this amount of time not only in Germany but also in all other countries to which the survivors returned. Even in Israel it was like that. The books by those who had sketched their stories directly after the war—Primo Levi, for example— remained lying in bookstores completely ignored for twenty years, until they were "discovered" at the end of the sixties and only then reissued in huge print runs, sold, and most likely read too, followed in the seventies by a veritable flood of novels, reports, documentations, and historical research "in the grand style" that continues unabated to this day.[8]

But since I *was* a Jew, I also wanted to be able to *say* it and to tell about me, my parents, and my grandparents—yes, my own story. I do not wish to assert that the beginning of writing actually has something to do with the theme being described, but certainly everyone who writes has his theme from the beginning—or, perhaps it is better to say, the theme has him. It does seem to me as if every writer, every artist, in fact, has only one theme, one single theme that he hides even from himself, sometimes well and sometimes not so well—a theme around which he circles his whole life long and which he cannot abandon. And when one finally sits down in front of the white paper and begins slowly to divide the light from the darkness and to bring order to the chaos, one has also decided to speak to the Other, as when one was a child and sometimes went up to another child and asked, "Will you be my friend?" One had to be very courageous to dare to make such a proposal, for one was asking not merely for a small friendship of three or four days, but for an eternal one that would withstand the tests of fire and water, and one wanted to tell the other the whole truth about oneself—to reveal oneself.

What was truly my story I had only suspected; it was a story that came from far away and was quite old. It was a story that had to do with impossible love, with the discrepancy between great expectations and the fulfillment of these expectations, with monstrous efforts and undertakings and with grasping at the wind. It was a story of the shattered hopes of my great-grandfather, my grandfather, and my father. This story is marked by existential experiences, by no means only Jewish ones, though perhaps they are more pronounced, more catastrophic, in the Jewish experience.

My great-grandfather, my grandfather, and my father had, as indicated, composed German books, and I stand here now and imitate them as if nothing had happened. Naturally, I judge their works very strictly: the ones by my great-grandfather are too pompous, those by my grandfather too assimilated, those by my father too subservient. They had spoken and written a lot, and it had all been for nothing. But perhaps the words they used had been the wrong ones and therefore futile. And now, if I too absolutely wanted to write again, I would have to speak with other words, different yet again, and start at the beginning. My first longer prose text I had called *Roman von einem Kinde* (*Novel of a Child*), probably for this very reason, although I had never known exactly why. The title came from pure intuition, and I only knew that it was right. Actually, the title has nothing at all to do with the content of the book, which is also not a novel but rather a collection of prose pieces. It has to do only with this attitude of starting from the very beginning, just like a child.

Perhaps that is also just a role. The role of the pioneer, however, is played out, and maybe a new path will open precisely from the helplessness. No one should think I am trying to acquiesce. Quite the opposite: I too want to speak about the "big things," only about them, about exile and deliverance, not in the language of the pioneers, who know everything and whose words carry their ideas before them, but rather in a way appropriate for the helpless person, who searches for the scattered memories and vague images swimming around inside him. These words he finds in everyday life; they would most likely be the banal words "from nothing," which are easily discarded and for that reason lying around everywhere anyway; one can collect them and (in accord with today's trend) recycle them.

The paradise of my forefathers, in the dreams of the better circles of the educated Breslau bourgeoisie, seems to me at any rate to be closed, and I must "set out upon the trip around the world and see if there is any back entrance."[9]

Before I started "really" to write—and by "really" I mean publishing books with well-known presses instead of writing plays that are never performed—I had removed myself from the

East and from Germany to France, although France was for me a foreign country in which I knew nobody, in which I had no connections or particular sympathies, and whose language I did not speak. I was much more of an Anglophile, and that not even out of any special knowledge of or love for England, but simply because England was the country that had taken my parents in and thereby saved their lives—thus out of love for my parents.

In this way, without any particular affection or dislike, France became the land of freedom for me. None of my forefathers had ever lived there, and it was thus easier there to start all over from the very beginning. Begin to be a "real" Jew and a "real" writer— I could also say begin "again."

I believe I am not harboring any particular illusions about these two aspects of my life, not about Judaism and not about literature.[10] I want to live with them in truth and not in lies, and I know perfectly well that there is no escape, no respite any-where, from this story about monstrous efforts and grasping at the wind, yet Judaism and writing became the center of my life in that other country. Precisely at the distant remove, as if only there could I finally begin to tell my own story in my own form. France was therefore already the "land of freedom," because there nobody was watching me, because I could live free from scrutiny and judgment, because the glance of the Other did not impart to me my shape and form. I would like to add, in order to pre-vent any fairy-tale ideas from arising, that this freedom rests above all on a lack of interest in the newcomer and is often dif-ficult to handle.

At some point along the way, however, I should have simply torn myself away "from the nest of familiar people, landscape, political relations, language, and security that I found there and which I knew I would never find again."[11] Previously, in Berlin, I lived among a circle of friends, of whom several, mostly men, were already writers or some other type of artist and whose es-cort I was allowed to be. Sometimes as a joke they called me the Gertrude Stein of Prenzlauer Berg, referring to the idea that I, so to speak, ran a salon, that I was a mediator, always available to discuss, criticize, and comment upon the poetry, plays, and other writings of my friends and to inspire them to further ideas and works. The fact that I was Jewish fit in especially well with this salon role; they could just as well have called me Rahel of Prenzlauer Berg, for, just like her, I was completely limited to my role as mediator; my own work consisted mainly of long letters and the staging of novels about unrequited love. My *Roman von einem Kinde* was a letter about an unhappy love and at the same time a farewell to those stagings and long letters.

I had taken on my role gladly and voluntarily, of course, and I do not accuse anybody of having prevented or delayed my relatively late "release." It took quite a while before I was able to separate or extricate myself from "my group," whose presence gave me security and a foothold but also burdened me with certain restrictions that I would sooner or later have to shake off. I had never dared to declare myself a writer before their eyes or, worse still, actually to write and to publish. For this reason, too, I had to distance myself and take on the difficult adventure of living in another country, even if it is only three blocks beyond the border.

We sit, then, on the other side of the Rhine and look across to Germany—"over there," as West Germans said for so long about the GDR. In the meantime, the wind has died down, and the Turkish child is absolutely insisting on playing ball with us again. I walk a ways and play with him, not because I long to play ball with children I don't know, but because I find doing so less stressful than explaining to his parents why we have no shop, less stressful than setting straight their picture of Jews—a picture that is apparently just as distorted as ours is of them—less stressful than clearing away all the misunderstandings that emerge between us in just this one afternoon and telling them the whole story of my great-grandfather, my grandfather, my father, and me.

TRANSLATED FROM THE GERMAN
BY MEGHAN W. BARNES

Notes

1. M. Braun, "Vorwort zu David Honigmann: Aufzeichnungen aus seinen Jugendjahren," *Jahrbuch für jüdische Geschichte und Literatur* 7 (1904).

2. Cf. Shulamit Volkov, *Jüdisches Leben und Antisemitismus im 19. u. 20. Jahrhundert* (Munich: Beck, 1990), 131–63, esp. 158 ff.

3. See Johannes Fuchs, "Der Internist und Medizinhistoriker Georg Honigmann: Krise und Reformbestrebungen in der Medizin bis gegen Ende der Weimarer Zeit," dissertation, Johannes-Gutenberg-Universität Mainz, 1993.

4. Barbara Honigmann, *Eine Liebe aus Nichts* (Berlin: Rowohlt, 1991), 93.

5. Ibid., 99.

6. Dan Diner, "Negative Symbiose," in *Babylon I* (Frankfurt am Main: Neue Kritik, 1986), 9–20, esp. 9.

7. Gerschom Scholem, "Juden und Deutsche," in *Judaica II* (Frankfurt am Main, 1970), 35.

8. For France, cf. Eric Conan, *Vichy, un passé qui ne passe pas* (Paris: Fayard, 1994), 9–30, esp. 20.

9. Heinrich von Kleist, "Über des Marionettentheater," (n.p.: 1810).

10. See David Honigmann, "Die deutsche Belletristik als Vorkämpferin der Judenemanzipation," in *Freihafen* (Altona, Germany: Hammerlich, 1844).

11. Honigmann, 48.

Song of the Jewish Princess

Michelene Wandor

Michelene Wandor was born in 1940 in London. She studied English at Cambridge, the sociology of literature at the University of Essex, and music at Trinity College of Music. Wandor says about her background: "I was born in England, of Russian-Polish parents, my substantive education and reading has been in English, and so 'English' literature is my imaginative spur. I am, therefore, a part of this history, but my placement in it is qualified in all sorts of ways. I am Jewish, I am a woman, I am a feminist and a socialist (whatever that means today), and some of my work has an 'avant-garde' element to it."

Wandor lives in London, where she is a playwright, poet, fiction writer, critic, and musician. She writes plays and dramatizations for BBC Radio and broadcasts on the arts, and she is a senior lecturer in creative writing at London Metropolitan University. Among her fiction and poetry are Guests in the Body *(1986);* Arky Types *(1987), with Sara Maitland;* Gardens of Eden *(1984);* Collected Poems *(1990); and* False Relations *(2004). Her study* Post-War British Drama: Looking Back in Gender *was published in 2001. She won an International Emmy for her adaptation of* The Belle of Amherst, *a play about Emily Dickinson, for television, and she has, with her group, the Siena Ensemble, produced a CD of the music of Salamone Rossi, the Jewish composer from Renaissance Mantua. Wandor comments on the situation of Jewish women writers in England: "We must, as writers, be free to choose our subject matter, our forms, but we also cannot forget who we are and what the cultural sources of our voices are. And I think that means — whatever our direct or indirect polemics are — that it is great when we 'write Jewish,' using the comfortable inflections, the characters, the situations, not censoring our Jewish voices. I would add here that this is hard to do in England. As women, as Jewish writers, we still have to fight to make our voices heard. We are heard a little better, but there is still a long way to go."*

❋

My thunderer blew in through the door, autumn leaves swirling behind him, green and brown scraps of the fading year barbed on the frayed strands of his wild woolen cloak, dry twigs pinned on his shoulders under the wide strap that held his bag, one lone leaf poised like a dancer on the brim of his hat.

Today, he who was always on time, he who always closed doors behind him, he who held himself carefully in his own space, today he was tousled, windswept, his cheeks red, his nose glowing and bulbous, his eyes wrinkled against the winter wind, his mouth taut with hurry and cold against the grin that I knew could warm his face. Well, he said, what are you waiting for?

I hushed my body's desire to rush to him and began to play.

I am the original Jewish princess. The authentic article. The instrument on which the real music, according to the text, can be played. Play me. I shall sound true to you.

It was a long day, stopping only for wine and bread and the bitter goat cheese Carlos had brought with him. He worked himself and us hard and did not talk to me, except to make points about the music. By early evening, I was shivering with tiredness and expectation. As we all walked through the cold stone halls to the Hall of Mirrors, I huddled into my own deep blue woolen cloak, the color of the evening summer sky. Coming in from the cold, the wave of heat in the hall hit me full in the face. The guests hardly noticed our arrival and scarcely nodded an ear in our direction as we began to play. As usual, Ferdinand and

Isabella talked throughout, though I knew that any flaw in the performance would invoke sarcasm the following day.

Halfway through the evening, some late guests arrived, and as the huge wooden doors were opened to admit them, the gusting wind blew out all the candles—except for two, one behind me and one behind Carlos. Momentarily the hall was in silence, and without any sense of preplanning, Carlos and I began playing our star piece of the evening; strings, wind, and voices flashed into the dark, and between verses Carlos and I improvised. For the first time that day he and I looked full at each other, our eyes, so alike, green flecked with brown, flashing across the hall, each lured by the pool of light behind the other's head. I swear that we invented fire that night. Flame spiraled and pirouetted between our notes, and for those few moments, the chatterers were silenced.

At the end, the ripples of music bowed their way into the corners of the hall, and we were applauded. Carlos nodded his head at me in approval and desire.

I can pick up any instrument and bow or pluck or blow and it will speak. My mother was the same. The bow cuts deep and springy into the string and I curve my body in reply.

When Carlos came into my room, he shut the door quietly and carefully. We still did not speak. Under my blue woolen cloak, his body felt as familiar to me as my own. His green eyes held mine, and as we deepened into each other, our movements fitted easily, as they always had.

Play me. I shall sound true to you.

Later we lay, my faced nuzzled into Carlos's armpit, smelling cloves and chamomile mixed with the acrid savor of satisfaction. There is something I must tell you, he said. I caught my breath. You're going back to her, I said. I knew it. It was only a matter of time.

He flipped himself over on top of me so that he could look at me. It isn't that, Isabella, he said. I began to cry. Every time I see you, I said, I feel it's for the last time. She won't let go. You can't leave the children. I hate goat cheese.

He put his hand over my mouth. I bit his fingers. Isabella, he said, you must listen. And then he whispered. He was late this morning because he had heard that before very long all infidels would be banished from Spain. I am Jewish, Isabella, he said softly, and you know what that means. I must leave before I am killed.

I stroked him. I knew you were Jewish, I said. Not just because of this—many men are circumcised in this world of mixed races. I just knew. You couldn't know, he said. Not in the way the Inquisition will know, not in the way—I interrupted: I'm coming with you, I said. No—he began. This time I put my hand over his mouth. Then I told him about my mother.

Never have an affair with a musician, she said. A scribe, a soldier, a goat farmer if you must, but not a musician. When I was tiny, she let me pluck the strings on her fiddle, showed me how she tightened the tension, let me hold the bow in my fat hand, and promised that one day I would be able to play as she did.

She was right about that, although she did not live to hear it. She also didn't live to see me disregard her advice about musicians. No doubt she would have smiled. My father, you see, was an itinerant musician, a man from North Africa, a Jew, a wandering minstrel who probably left behind him as many children as musical memories. He came to our village one night, in the height of summer. My mother's husband was away in the mountains, with the goats. It was late, no one saw him arrive. My mother gave him shelter. He played to her. The next morning he wrapped his *ud,* the instrument, which is so like the courtly lute that every amateur plays here, and he disappeared. My mother described his fingers like spiderwebs, trailing and caressing the strings, no frets to hurdle the fingers, allowing him to bend their tunes to his will. He was dark skinned. With green eyes.

My mother told me all this the night before she died. The soldiers came looking for infidels. My mother was Jewish, but she thought no one knew. She told me the story about my father, gave me her blue woolen cloak, and made me go and hide with the goats. Her charred body was flung on the ground some days later. I think about her often. I wonder how long it took for the thick earth to rot her flesh. I prefer to think about that than to wonder what the Inquisition did to her. I also worry because I cannot remember the color of her eyes.

When a string is ready to snap, it plays sharper and sharper. It cries for the attention that can do it no good. My life is fraying at the edges. I began not to sound true to myself.

The following afternoon, two musicians, carrying instruments, strolled toward the town walls. Carlos and I also each carried a small vial of poison. His alchemist friend assured him that anyone who took it would fall asleep long before the poison began to eat them away. We promised each other through our tears that we would rather die than be subjected to torture.

The soldiers on guard by the town walls laughed and applauded as we cavorted with our fiddles, mad court musicians aping their wandering minstrel brethren, a lower caste, vulgar and uncertain and despicable. So harmless and silly were we that they allowed us to wander through the gates and serenade a flock of goats herded on a hill opposite.

I have left my texts behind me.

We slept in a field. Next day, lulled by the quiet of the countryside, we were reckless. A small town, sleepy in the early afternoon haze, suddenly came alive with shouts and screams. Soldiers and locals chased a small group of people—men, women, and children. An old man tripped and fell just beyond the entrance to the alley in which we hid. The crowd kicked him bloody and limp. Then they hurtled past us, knocking us aside, and when they had passed, Carlos was no longer with me. I waited, huddled in an abandoned house, hoping he would come back. When it was dark I searched a little. The streets were strewn with dead and wounded. No one dared to touch them. I dared not stay.

I have had to learn how to improvise all over again.

Memory can be kind. I remember endless roads and fields, green streaked with brown, brown with green. I could not eat. I felt sick all the time. My fiddle opened doors to me, gave me beds and food. I took it all and more often than not gave it to the next beggar I met on my way. I searched every face for the familiar mouth, for the green eyes. I learned that northern Italy—Mantova, Ferrara, Venezia even—were the places to go. I hardly noticed that my periods seemed to have stopped. The road changed everything. In any case, the real me was somewhere else, with a man whose hair curled over his collar, whose crooked nose could wrinkle in glee, whose eyes were like mine.

When I finally cried, my imagination flooded out of me. I bled for four days as I had never bled before. Now I knew that Carlos and his child were gone from me forever. To the rest of the world, he had never been. To me, he could never be again; neither cloaked in rage nor clear in love. Just misty in my music as I played.

My text comes from the heart. Nothing can be more authentic.

Giovanni has brown eyes. He is kind. He is good. He is my rock. He is calm and decisive, and he waits for me to love him. I should love him. I am grateful to him. After all, he picked me out, a grubby, weary, wandering minstrel, traveling round Italy, playing anywhere, and he made me into the highest in the land—in the region, anyway. I am the duchess. Of course, no one knows that I am Jewish. Merely that I am Spanish. I speak Italian impeccably, but with a soft, sibilant accent. When I am asked when I left Spain, I say 1490; if I told then the true year, 1492, they might associate it with the expulsion of the Jews and wonder.

Giovanni is much older than I am. His first wife died in childbirth. The son, a wayward child, was sent to fight with Giovanni's mercenary army against the Turks. Make a man of him, they said. When he returns, he will be Giovanni's heir. So it does not matter that I do not seem able to conceive. I can make love when Giovanni desires, except that for me there is no love in it, just gratitude.

I ached so much from wandering. I had to stop. This seemed the only way. Here I continue to play as I please. My musicians are the finest in the region, envied by the whole of northern Italy. I even pay them on time.

When my strings have settled, you can play me. Then I shall sound true to you.

And then, on a rough, blustery winter day, Carlo came home. Here in the north, in the vast, flat plain, on the river that flows to the sea, it rains and rains. Nothing is ever free of mud.

The concert was almost over. I played in the last piece. Just as we were about to begin, the door burst open and a young man thundered in, bringing gusting rain and leaves with him, cloak flung over one shoulder, rough boots, a crooked nose, hair curling down over his shoulders.

I played just for him, my heart pounding, my arm quivering, my sound small and sweet. His eyes were on me the whole time, burning me in tune.

Every text contains within it the music of a thousand others.

The next day Carlo came to see me. A young man, weathered, with no sign of the previous night's thunderer. Teach me to play, he said. Teach me to play like you. He looked at me and in his eyes I saw Carlos again, and the baby I had never known, and something else, someone new, whose body was as familiar as my own and whom I could not touch except strictly in the line of duty, to show how to balance the instrument, to show how to hold the bow, how to flex the wrist, how to find the notes.

He was an exemplary pupil. He rewarded my efforts by working hard and throwing himself into the music like a child. He hated being a soldier, he told me. He was not going to be a ruler. He wanted to be a wandering minstrel, to go on the road, to live free of all ties and responsibilities. I teased him. You're too spoiled, I said. And I gave him the most fiendish musical exercise I could conjure up, as if that would keep him with me for longer.

Let us play our texts to each other. Perhaps we shall sound true.

There was nothing I can think of that precipitated the crisis. One day he blundered through everything, careless, discordant, sullen. When he finished I exploded. Why? He flung his bow on the ground. You, he said. I cannot play to you. You create the conditions of performance. Who do you think you are? You make me nervous.

I am your audience, I said. If you can play to me, you can play to anyone. I can't play to you, he said. Then you'll never make it on the road, I taunted. Music happens because of you, not because of the road. But you're such a natural, he said. Who taught you? No one, I said. I taught myself. I learned as I traveled. I learned as I played in fields and I learned as I played in courts. You're the real thing, he said, the authentic article.

He said it with sadness, his shoulders drooped, his back bowed, his legs apart, his elbows on his knees, his fingers clamped together in a double fist. A lock of hair fell forward over his face. I lifted it and one finger brushed his cheek. He looked up, his eyes green, just like mine.

I am newly strung, with fine gut, translucent, springy. Play me. I dare you.

What can I tell you? That in the moonlight, in the haven of my tower room, the room of my music, his body felt more familiar than my own? That his skin was warm where mine was cool, and mine warm where his was cool? That we fitted easily until we were the same temperature and could not tell who was who, and he was not Carlos, and he was not a baby, and he was not my stepson, and I did not know who he was?

You have everything you want, he said, his cheek against my breast. You have a husband who adores you. You are gifted. You are beautiful. Guilty, my young lord, I said. Don't call me young, he said sharply. I am sorry, I said, my hand on his belly, where the pulses fluttered. I stroked him calm. You know nothing about me, I said. I have heard you play, he said. That is enough.

I am not what I seem, I said. I don't care, he said, I should have married you. I cried and he kissed my face. He smelled of cloves and rosemary and permanence.

And then the door was kicked down.

It takes only a split second to snap. Much longer to be tuned.

Tonight I shall take poison. I shall go out into the dark. I shall cross the river by the small stone bridge that curves over the water at an angle. I shall turn right on the opposite bank and walk along by the river for a few paces until I am opposite the tower in which Carlo and I made love.

I am taut.

The guards let me have my fiddle this evening. They think my husband is wrong to have his adulterous wife beheaded. I think he is wrong too, but he knows that he has no alternative at his own court. If he let me live, he would have to face me every day and see his son in my eyes.

The guards have brought me my cloak and the cushion on

which Carlo and I lay. I shall put the cushion between me and the cold, damp stone. I shall wrap myself in my deep blue cloak. I shall drink the poison. I shall fall asleep before it begins to tear me apart.

I am the real thing. The first Jewish princess. The authentic instrument on which the musical text can be played. Play me. I shall sound true to you.

In sunlight the river is green. My mother's eyes were green.

Acknowledgments

We would like to offer our thanks to all the authors who have contributed to this volume as well as to the Jewish studies program at Wellesley College for its generous support of this publication.

Thanks are also due to all the translators of the texts included in our anthology as well as to Antony Polonsky for his counsel and to Emily Coit for her editorial work.

Rebecca Gruber, Miriam Levine, Vivian Liska, and, last but not least, Sandy Nolden have read drafts of the introduction and generously provided critical insight.

"On the Edge of the World" is translated by permission of the author. Original contribution to this volume.

"Exotic Birds" is reprinted from *The House of Memory: Stories by Jewish Women Writers of Latin America*. Edited by Marjorie Agosín. New York: Feminist Press at the City University of New York, 1999. Copyright © 1999 by Marjorie Agosín. Reprinted by permission of the Feminist Press at the City University of New York, www.feministpress.org.

"Beyond the Bridges" is reprinted from *Insiders and Outsiders: Jewish and Gentile Culture in Germany and Austria*. Edited by Dagmar C. G. Lorenz and Gabriele Weinberger. Detroit: Wayne State University Press, 1994. Reprinted by permission of the publisher.

"A Yiddish Writer Who Writes in French" is used by permission of the author. French original published in *Pardès* 21 (1995): 237–41.

"Jews" is reprinted from Clara Sereni, *Eppure.* Milan: Feltrinelli, 1995. Translated and reprinted by permission of the publisher.

"March 1953" is reprinted from *Glas: New Russian Writing.* Brookline, Mass.: Zephyr Press, 1994: 6. Reprinted by permission of the publisher.

"Holy Fire" is reprinted from Carl Friedman, *The Gray Lover: Three Stories.* Translated by Jeannette K. Ringold. New York: Persea Books, 1998. Translation copyright © 1998 by Persea Books, Inc. Reprinted by permission of the publisher.

"On My Great-Grandfather, My Grandfather, My Father, and Me" is reprinted from *World Literature Today* (summer 1995). Used by permission of the author.

"Song of the Jewish Princess" copyright © 1989 by Michelene Wandor. Reprinted by permission of the author.

Thomas Nolden is the director of the comparative literature program at Wellesley College and the author of several books on contemporary Jewish literature in Germany, Austria, and France.

Frances Malino is the Sophia Moses Robison Professor of Jewish Studies and History at Wellesley College and the chair of the Jewish studies program. She is the author of *The Sephardic Jews of Bordeaux: Assimilation and Emancipation in Revolutionary and Napoleonic France* and *A Jew in the French Revolution: The Life of Zalkind Hourwitz.*

Jewish Lives

For a complete list of titles, see the Northwestern University Press Web site at www.nupress.northwestern.edu.